Into the Beyond

Part III : Fires of Heaven

Into the Beyond

Part III : Fires of Heaven

Paul James Keyes

ISBN 978-1-952872-03-7

Published in the United States by Verge Publishing.
VergePublishing.org

Cover artwork by Paul James Keyes and Raven Wade Keyes.
Internal design by Paul James Keyes.

This is a work of fiction. Names, characters, places, and
incidents either are the product of the author's imagination or
are used fictitiously. Any resemblance to actual persons, living
or dead, events, or locales is entirely coincidental.

You can follow Paul on Twitter **@PaulJKeyes**,
TikTok **@PaulJamesKeyes**,
or visit **VergePublishing.org** to become an honorary
Chosen!

For Raven,
The Josie to my Lewis.

Table of Contents

The Beyond exists outside of time…
the *Fires of Heaven* burn across the ages.

Angels wept the day the heavens burned. The mortal realm stood in awe as the glow of the flames bled through into our sky. We laid out on blankets, pointing up at the shimmering glow, unknowing. If only our eyes had been aimed lower, perhaps we would have seen that the terrors held to the fringes no longer.

CHAPTER

1

Trauma

"Five years?" asked Luna, gawking incredulously at Harvey from the passenger seat.

Harvey grimaced slightly. He kept his eyes on the road as he chose a careful response. "I mean… yeah… we still have the debt from the new furnace to pay off, and then the roof is going to need replacing within the next couple of years… it's not cheap."

"It's not a ten year anniversary vacation if you take it thirteen years into the marriage!"

Harvey's eyes flicked over to Luna for a moment, judging the level of irritation visible on her face before returning to the road. "It's not like I don't want to take you places," he said. "I just don't see how we can save up enough for a decent trip when we're living paycheck to paycheck still and have all these big expenses coming up.   Airfare alone costs a fortune…."

"You do realize Jo will be fourteen in five years? A teenager already, Harvey.   She needs to experience things—go on trips—become more cultured! We always said we didn't want to go to Europe when she was younger because she wouldn't really remember it, but now it's a different excuse. We need to make memories!"

Harvey glanced back at their nine-year-old daughter through the rearview mirror. Her high Native American cheekbones were becoming more and more prominent as she lost her baby fat. She was the spitting image of her beautiful mother. Josie was sitting quietly, staring out the window with an absent expression on her face—just watching the snowflakes as they streamed by sideways through the darkness outside the car.

"I don't want to talk about this in front of her," said Harvey. He sighed. "I'm already putting in these extra hours at work. You know that. What would you have me do? Let the roof rot off and blow away before I get it fixed? I want to make memories too, but my first job is literally to keep a roof over our heads."

Luna turned in her seat and placed a hand on Josie's knee. "Josie, Honey, could you put your headphones in for a little bit? Mommy and Daddy need to talk about boring adult stuff."

Josie turned towards her mother, and then slowly shifted her head to stare questioningly at the empty seat beside her. It was odd behavior—she couldn't have missed the headphones hanging out of the seat pocket directly in front of her, clearly visible.

Luna reached around awkwardly and retrieved them for Josie. She dangled them out in front of her. "Right here, Honey."

Josie smiled briefly at the empty car seat before turning back towards her mother and accepting the headphones with an outstretched hand. "Adeona says not to fight."

Harvey swerved the car slightly as he glanced back again. "Adeona?" he asked.

"It's her imaginary friend," said Luna. "She's been talking about her for a few weeks now. You'd know that if you ever paid any attention."

The car skidded slightly as Harvey jerked the wheel with a tightened grip. "Which is it? Do you want me to work harder or work less? I can't do both at the same time. You know how work drains me."

"Adeona says—"

"—You act like I'm not working hard every day on my feet, too," said Luna. "I'm asking you to be present with Josie. I manage it."

"Adeona says you guys—"

"That's not a fair comparison—"

"ADEONA SAYS you guys shouldn't fight tonight!" Josie yelled over them, finally getting their attention. "She says to remember why you love each other, because each day is a gift and you shouldn't take it for granted."

Harvey looked at her through the rearview mirror again. Luna craned her head back around too, locking sad eyes upon her daughter for a moment. She gazed over at Harvey next, studying the side of his head. His jaw was clenched tight, fighting back more biting words. His focus remained on the winding road ahead, but his eyes soon softened.

They both knew the bickering needed to stop. Josie was sensitive, always reflecting the mood of the room back with a bleeding heart. They usually did better about hiding their occasional fights.

Harvey sighed. "She's right," he admitted. "You girls are my whole world. We're both fighting for the exact same thing—to make our lives better—for our future."

Luna's mouth twitched up into a half-smile. "I'm sorry," she said. "I'm just sick of living for tomorrow. I want it to start now."

"Kiss him," Josie ordered, eyes wide open, staring up at them with the most serious expression a nine-year-old could command.

Luna couldn't squash her smile any longer; their love was too strong. She leaned in slowly and planted a loud, wet kiss on Harvey's cheek, complete with audible kissing sound effect.

Harvey laughed. "One more," he said, shifting his head sideways to present his cheek again. As Luna moved towards him, he quickly turned to face her, forcing their lips to meet in a brief, stolen kiss. Luna wiped her mouth with the back of her hand in feigned disgust.

They were still thirty minutes out from the main highway, heading home from a skiing trip that was intended to refresh their overworked bodies and minds. The weekend had ended up feeling more like a workout than a vacation.

Harvey powered on the radio and flipped through the stations until he found one playing Christmas music. They were supposed to be having fun, after all. The Carpenters' version of *Sleigh Ride* played out through the speakers, interrupted by brief bits of static from the spotty mountain reception. Luna leaned her head over onto Harvey's shoulder, enjoying the dance of the snowdrifts outside. Poofs of white swirled back and forth across the roadway, blustering up through their headlight beams like tiny tornados of snow.

As they rounded a gradual curve into the final downgrade stretch before the lowlands, Josie quietly unbuckled her seatbelt and stood up, hunched awkwardly in the middle of the backseat.

Neither Harvey nor Luna noticed her at first. Josie stood silently with her eyes closed and her arms spread wide, as if she could feel the cold air on the outside of the car rushing over her. Luna was the first to realize that something was amiss. She glanced in the passenger-side mirror and saw an empty seat where Josie should have been. She spun around immediately to see what was going on.

"Josie!" she cried out, shocked by the strange pose. "What are you doing? Sit down!"

Harvey turned his head back as well, unamused by Josie's antics. "That's dangerous!" he cried out. The car swerved again. He whipped back around to face the road, but it was too late. The tires began to skid as the icy shoulder took ahold of the vehicle. Trying to regain control of the slide, Harvey turned the wheel back in the opposite direction, but the car continued to drift slightly off-kilter.

Harvey's knuckles grew white as he clutched the steering wheel with all his might.

Luna screamed.

A bright light filled Josie's vision. The low horn of a semi-truck blared. A moment later, her feet lifted off the seat. She was weightless, floating through the air with an effortless spin. Bits of glass stung like hot oil as they collided with her face. Grinding metal roared behind her in a thundering rumble as the frozen wind blew her hair back wildly. One second she was soaring head over heels, and then the next, the crystalline snowbank had consumed her whole. A plume of fresh powder rose up in a cloud like a trailing wake as she tumbled free of the carnage on the narrow pass.

***

Josie Mays sat up in bed, waking with a start. Her whole body was drenched in sweat.

The same damn dream again....

It had repeated often over the last five years.

She knew that night would be with her forever. She would never forget what she had done, nor forgive herself for it. Parts of her wished she could forget the whole night—just erase it from her memory—but she clutched to it all the same. It was her last and most vivid memory of her parents.

Josie rubbed her face, pushing her dampened hair off her forehead. The sounds of the other campers sleeping in the surrounding bunks was disconcerting for a moment before she remembered where she was—Camp Orkila, doing an extended teen summer camp program. The other girls were all mostly fast asleep, faces turned towards the walls as the first gray light of morning came pouring in through the cabin's singular window.

Channie Davis was the exception—she looked like a dark silhouette as she leaned against the windowsill, staring out into the early morning gloom. She turned her head to look back at Josie, but didn't say anything before returning her gaze to the window.

Josie wafted her night-shirt up and down, trying to bring cooler air to her overheated skin. The un-air-conditioned cabin was making her nightmares flair up worse than usual. She could still hear the wind howling in her dark, icy world. The grinding of metal and the crinkling of glass—to her, it was akin to the sound of snapping bones.

That night, her world had changed irreparably.

Today, it would change again.

"There's someone watching our cabin from within the woods," said Channie, her eyes still locked on the window. "He's been standing there since before I woke up."

Josie wasn't sure Channie was speaking to her at first, but after glancing around more thoroughly she realized she was the only other girl awake.

"He's so tall…" said Channie.

Josie blinked several times and rubbed the sleep from her eyes before standing up and joining her at the window. The girl pointed quietly into the dark woods about one-hundred yards out, beyond the cabin's clearing. Josie squinted, searching for a human shape. "I don't see anything," she said.

Channie glanced at her again to check where she was looking, then pointed a little farther to the left. "Right there."

Josie shifted her gaze accordingly across the shadows of the tree trunks. A skinny tree, shorter than the rest, leaning slightly against the wind, caught her attention. She narrowed her eyes. It was too tall to be anything but a tree, but it did have an eerie silhouette—it almost looked like it had shoulders and a head…. She scanned her eyes across the region several more times without seeing anything else before her focus returned to the odd shape once again.

Josie continued to watch the shadow in silence with Channie for some time, certain that it was no more than their wild imaginations playing tricks on their eyes… that is… until Channie whimpered a fearful gasp and the too-tall form slowly receded into the forest.

Hello everyone, Mr. Gray here. Poor Josie… she really was unjustly traumatized as a child wasn't she? It's a wide, cruel multi-verse out there… Josie's path is important, though it does feel like she keeps moving between a rock and a hard place. The Agares are to blame ultimately, so don't take it out on us Parcae! They want to eliminate Josie and everyone else that becomes important to the future of humanity. There's only one path forward that doesn't lead to disaster, so wish her luck and stay tuned!

Keep vigilant,

-Mr. Gray

CHAPTER

2

Scare Tactics

"It was probably just one of the boys trying to scare you," said Rebecca Kwon as she shoveled a heaping fork-load of hash-browns into her mouth.

Josie shook her head. "It had to be at least eight feet tall," she said.

"They probably were just on a ladder or something, wearing a costume."

"That doesn't make any sense…" Josie insisted. "The way it moved… it couldn't have been a ladder—"

"—Or something like that, you know what I mean," said Rebecca. "It was just the boys pulling a prank. That's what they do. You can't let it scare you."

Channie was sitting on the opposite side of the mess hall, her cheeks still ghostly pale. She refused to talk about what they'd seen. None of the other girls believed Josie's story without Channie's corroboration.

For Josie, seeing something that no one else believed existed was triggering. Her experience with Adeona left her doubting her own sanity. Her grandfather and all the therapists she'd seen over the last five years insisted that the accident had not been her fault, but Josie knew there were only two possibilities: Either Adeona only existed inside her head and Josie was entirely responsible for her parent's deaths or else Adeona really was real and the fact that Josie listened to the little demon still made her responsible for the accident in an only slightly less direct way. She was guilty regardless of which possibility she chose, and also possibly insane.

Deep down, Josie knew she hadn't been making up Adeona. She'd never had invisible friends before or after the Parca came to her with her silly little games that led to ultimate disaster. There were things in the world that existed beyond human understanding. Channie had seen the tall man too, even if she wouldn't admit to it now. Her fear was real.

"Pass the ketchup," said Rebecca.

Josie glanced down at her own breakfast, still untouched, and then over at the red squeeze bottle. She pushed it closer to Rebecca.

Across the mess hall, one of the camp counselors, Matt Greene, was setting up a step stool to hang a banner from the crossbeam that ran the length of the room. The outdoorsman led the water-sports activities as well as manning the climbing wall—anything that required muscle. He unhooked his belt knife, still in its leather sheath, and placed it on a nearby table before stepping up to the top of the stool.

"Did you see Steph's goat?" asked Rebecca with a scoff. "She wants it to be our cabin's mascot."

Josie stood up, her eyes locked on Matt's knife.

Rebecca looked at her oddly.

"Follow me," said Josie. She didn't wait, setting off immediately across the long room.

"What about your breakfast?" asked Rebecca. She hopped up, snatching Josie's bacon off her plate before following her through the mess hall.

Josie paused briefly to let Rebecca catch up. "Block his sight," she said to her, gesturing towards Matt. The counselor was still fiddling with a roll of duct tape.

Rebecca stared at her with wide eyes, but then stood between her and Matt. Josie walked past the table, grabbing the knife as she went.

Channie, seated nearby, watched them both with a blank expression as Josie shoved the weapon under her shirt and continued on, straight out of the building. Rebecca's black ponytail bounced back and forth as she ran after Josie.

Josie stepped around the side of the building. The leather sheath felt warm against her skin as she slipped it down the inside of her pants. She hooked it over her belt and adjusted it to sit snugly against her outer thigh.

Rebecca's mouth turned down into a frown "What are you going to do with that?" she asked.

"It's just a precaution," said Josie. There was no point in explaining why she felt the need to steal the knife. No one else apart from Channie could possibly understand her worries.

The rattling of a bell caught both of their attentions. A white goat on a leash, led by Stephanie Bennett, jingled into view from around the front of the building. It was gnawing relentlessly on a red bandana that the irritating blonde had tied loosely around its neck. The goat's bug-eyed stare landed across Josie and Rebecca—one eye seemingly on each of them at the same time. The goat's awkward gaze drew Steph to notice them as well.

Steph's expression soured, but she immediately changed her course to approach them. She thrust a clipboard with a list of signatures on it out towards them. "Sign this petition to make Jerry the official mascot of Red Cabin."

"You named the goat Jerry?" asked Josie.

"Obviously," said Steph.

Jerry tried to nibble on Rebecca's pant leg.

"We aren't signing anything," said Rebecca, yanking her leg back. "No one wants your stupid goat to be our mascot." Steph and Rebecca had been feuding since day one of camp when Steph made fun of Rebecca for not knowing how to apply eyeliner.

"Sign it or I'll tell everyone you were doing drugs back here," threatened Steph.

Rebecca snatched the clipboard out of Steph's hand and threw it as hard as she could down the side of the building. It landed with a splat in a patch of muddy grass.

Steph's face grew red with anger. She was tall and skinny, but still had more muscle mass than Rebecca. She lunged at her, dropping Jerry's leash in the process. Rebecca and Steph went to the ground immediately, tussling about. Jerry stared ahead mindlessly, unperturbed by the fight. He began chewing on his bandana once again.

Josie joined the fray, attempting to pull Steph off of Rebecca, but she got kicked painfully in the ribs for her trouble. The two girls screeched unintelligibly back and forth, rolling around and pulling each other's hair until Steph gained control and sat on top of the smaller Korean girl.

Rebecca scrunched her face up as Steph raised her fist, preparing to rain blows down against her.

Josie had to act fast.

She drew the belt knife out of her pants and gestured threateningly at Steph. "Do it and I'll cut you," she said, maintaining as calm a voice as she could.

Steph's eyes grew wide with fear as she looked up at the knife. She started crying immediately. She shifted backwards off Rebecca, hopped back up to her feet, and immediately ran away.

Rebecca's ponytail was askew, but she wasn't hurt. "Stupid goat," she muttered under her breath.

Josie wasn't sure if she was referring to Jerry or Steph.

"*Meh-eh-eh!*" Jerry bleated.

"We should go…" said Josie.

They ran off towards the woods before Steph could find a counselor to tell on them.

Steph and her goat.... I've got to admit, the silly fella really is starting to gnaw *at my heartstrings! Even Jerry's path is complicated and important. It's all undoubtedly ridiculous, unlikely, and ever so necessary to the grand design of my plan. So much hangs in the balance....*

Keep vigilant,

-Mr. Gray

CHAPTER

3

Operation Save Jerry (the goat)

"I'm outside your front door!" read the text from Steph.

Channie sat up in bed and glanced out the window. It was already after midnight. She hadn't spoken to Steph for the better part of a year, and now suddenly here she was, out of the blue, on the doorstep of Channie's mom's house. The skinny blonde looked uncomfortable as she shifted her gaze between her phone, waiting for Channie's response, and the dark street behind her. Steph's arms were full of plastic grocery bags, handles stretched thin under the weight of their contents against her fuzzy white hoodie.

"Just stay quiet, my mom's asleep. Be there in a bit," Channie texted back. She crept to the stairs and down them in silence. She had a bad feeling in her gut as she carefully opened the front door and joined Steph on the porch.

"I need your help contacting *Mr. Gray*," Steph said quietly, skipping over greetings and pleasantries and all the months of radio silence between them.

Channie stared back at Steph incredulously. The creature she spoke of—Mr. Gray—was a mischievous, doll-sized, time-traveling fortune teller that they'd had run-ins with in the past. He was a Parca—plural, Parcae—or Fate: A member of a tiny, ageless species; manipulators of destiny; denizens of a place outside of time itself, known as the Beyond. Channie's mom would have called Mr. Gray a demon. She would have been horrified to learn that Channie knew how to contact him.

Steph took in Channie's reluctant expression. "Please! This is important," she said. "I need to use Mr. Gray's portals to go back in time and save Jerry."

Channie choked slightly on her spit. "The goat?" she asked.

Steph nodded enthusiastically, a gleam of wild energy in her eyes.

Channie crossed her arms. "You want to go back in time six years to our most terrible experience in life—one from which we both barely escaped with our lives—just to try to save a goat." It was a statement, not a question, and it was jam-packed full of judgmental undertone.

"My 'most terrible experience'?" Steph chuckled softly. "Speak for yourself—I dated Landon."

Channie cringed. She too had dated Landon, more recently than Steph. That was over now. They both were well aware of their shared history, although Steph had no idea of the true extent of Channie's relationship with Landon. It had gone on for over a year, completely in secret, before they revealed the relationship to anyone in their friends group. Channie had consoled Landon when he was freshly out of Steph's arms… *mostly* out of Steph's arms, anyway….

Channie glanced down again at the armful of grocery bags looped across Steph's wrists and fingers—they were so heavy that her fingertips were starting to turn red. The subtle stink of butchered meat was quickly leaching through the plastic and out into the night air. "Please don't tell me that's a bunch of goat meat…."

Steph grinned through gritted teeth. "I need to switch it with Jerry to keep the timeline consistent. I remember seeing a torn up body."

Six years ago, when they were young teens, they'd briefly seen Jerry's remains after he was devoured by blood-sucking ghasts that attacked their summer camp—it had been their first supernatural experience, intertwining their fates.

"This has been weighing on me," Steph pouted. She lowered her bags, placing them in a pile beside the door.

Channie wasn't sure if she meant that the meat was literally heavy or that Jerry's death had been weighing on her for all these years. "Do you not find it kinda messed up trading one goat's life for another? And aren't you a vegetarian?"

"Vegan." Steph rolled her eyes. "Whatever, this goat was already dead."

Channie wasn't about to back down. "But you're contributing to the demand for goat butchery. The industrial meat market will slaughter more goats in the future because of the increased demand. You're trading a life for a life."

Steph scoffed. "A goat life. A future goat life. That's the moral ground you're trying to stand on?" She shook her head in disappointment. "One—I knew Jerry. I didn't know this other goat. And two—my tiny contribution to the industrial meat market isn't going to make a blip in actually changing any decision made about anything to do with how many goats are raised for slaughter in the future. I don't have that power. And I already bought the meat, so let's get past this already and not let it go to waste! And besides, you know Jerry would have done it for either one of us!"

Channie had a strange tingle in her stomach—a nervous twinge. She stared back at Steph with her jaw hanging open. "Okay, fine," she said despite her better judgment, "but let's make this quick."

Steph drove a baby blue new style Volkswagen Beetle. Channie was already regretting her decision to help as they took off down the street and made their way towards the freeway. Poppy, electronic dance music thudded from the car's stereo. Steph, in high spirits, wiggled slightly in her seat, dancing along to the music with her shoulders.

Channie yawned widely. She had been about to go to sleep before Steph's unexpected arrival.

"I already wrote the note for Mr. Gray," said Steph. "I just couldn't remember which tree the time pocket was in."

Time pockets were invisible pockets of space that existed outside of time. Eddies in the river of time. Items put into them could be retrieved in the past or the future. It was confusing and weird, but placing a note inside the time pocket they knew about was the easiest way to get in touch with Mr. Gray.

The odd creature must have frequented the pocket at some point in history. At the current time, it was situated under a gap made by an exposed tree root growing up over the topsoil deep within a city park in Edmonds, Washington, about thirty minutes south of Channie's mom's house in Everett.

Between songs, a rustling of plastic bags sounded from the backseat. A look of concern appeared in Steph's eyes as she noticed the curious crinkles. She glanced in the rear view mirror and then quickly twisted in place to look behind her.

"Which bag has the snacks in it?" came a high-pitched voice from the backseat.

Steph slammed on the brakes.

Channie screamed as the car continued to slide, drifting off the road towards a utility pole.

Steph screamed, knuckles turning white against the steering wheel as she turned back around.

Their seatbelts locked.

Mr. Gray squealed, rocketing unrestrained through the air with all the bags of goat meat into the front seat. His tiny, gangly legs flopped around, bumping into the stereo system, turning the volume knob to max.

The beat dropped in the music as the car lurched to a halt, inches from colliding with the pole.

Channie's heart was pounding in her chest along with the beat of the music.

Steph quickly cranked the volume back down. A nervous laughter escaped from her like a chattering bird.

Channie let out a deep breath that she hadn't realized she was holding. She soon joined in with her own manic laughter.

The relief was short lived.

Everything lit up suddenly inside the car—piercing fluorescent headlights pouring in. A truck horn blared. Steph and Channie both screamed again. The whole car shook as the truck barreled past, too close for comfort.

"We're all fine," said Mr. Gray, standing up on the center console. "No need to panic. It doesn't hit us, obviously." His eyes shined like a cats, reflecting red in the darkness.

Steph turned on the cab light. Both girls watched Mr. Gray as he brushed off the little button-down suit he always wore— it was a patchwork mess that looked like a bunch of cloth swatches sewn together. Bits of the patches stuck out along many of the sew lines, giving the pale skin creature a disheveled appearance.

"How long have you—?" Channie started, but trailed off from the pointless question. Mr. Gray was magical. Channie learned long ago not to fret over the how's or why's. Her hands shook softly—adrenaline lingering with no clear direction to take her.

Steph rummaged through her purse and retrieved the note she had prepared to place into the time pocket.

"I already know of your quest," said Mr. Gray without looking at the note. "Other versions of you have wanted to save that goat. You always make the same request. I came preemptively. The Agares are watching over some time pockets now. It's not safe to use them for communication."

Channie's heart beat faster at the mention of the Agares. An inter-dimensional war was raging outside of—and all across— time, perpetuated by the Agares' thirst to repurpose the energy of countless universes to fuel their own. It meant a slow, cold death for Earth and many other realms if the Agares succeeded. Most humans were blissfully unaware of all of this, but Channie and Steph knew the stakes. The Agares were not small like the Parcae. They were up to twelve feet tall with slender limbs, and although they often stood upright like a human, they could move terrifyingly fast on all fours. They were the ones who sent the vampiric ghasts to kill Channie and her friends—and Jerry, indirectly—at summer camp all those years before.

Mr. Gray told them both previously that they were destined to oppose the Agares' agenda.

Lucky us, thought Channie, rolling her eyes while no one was looking. She envied the carefree existence everyone else got to scoot around living. She knew the truth about the things that lurked beyond the fringes of science. So much more existed than anyone knew. She couldn't be carefree. She had to worry about the Agares literally erasing her. They could do that—erase people—with energy weapons. People ceased to have ever existed when struck, evaporated and forgotten by everyone who ever knew them. The Agares were working to end the universe.

"So you'll help us?" asked Steph.

Mr. Gray licked his thin lips as he straightened his black stringy hair. "Your task is pointless," he said, "but I know your feelings on this matter, so I'll ferry you there and back in exchange for the calories in your snack bag." He began to rustle through the plastic bags again until he found the only one that didn't contain goat meat. He pulled a package of wafer cookies out, his little fingers working fast to tear open the foil and yank the plastic tray free. He'd already munched down three cookies before Steph could respond.

"I don't mind sharing," she said. "I bought those for the drive."

Mr. Gray didn't stop chewing as he smiled. "That's why I arrived before you ate them."

Channie was having doubts about the task ahead. Mr. Gray thought it was pointless too… but he also wasn't stopping them.

"I'll keep you both safe," said Mr. Gray, "as long as you listen to my every instruction."

Steph squealed with joy and squeezed Mr. Gray in a tight hug. The Parca grunted. Steph plopped him back down on the center console. Mr. Gray straightened out his suit again.

Another car passed around them, honking

Steph returned her attention to the road. She backed away from the pole and then pulled off into the nearest abandoned parking lot.

Mr. Gray spoke for only Channie to hear while Steph was distracted. "The goat isn't important, but neither one of us is talking her out of this. It goes best if we just indulge her."

Channie was still scared, but she felt her heart soften as she thought about how much Jerry must have meant to Steph if she was still thinking about him six years after his death.

Everyone exited the car. Channie helped Steph gather all the goat meat and then joined Mr. Gray off to the side.

He waved an outstretched hand through the air, gesturing for a portal to materialize. Wisps of smoke condensed in the air, swirling around the invisible doorway. The space seemed to deaden, making the distant strip mall behind it appear hazy to the eye.

"It's ready," said Mr. Gray, looking up at Steph.

Steph's expression was steely eyed. She didn't hesitate as she walked through the opening and into the Beyond.

Channie waited until Steph vanished from sight. "This is going to be stupid and dangerous for no reason, isn't it?"

Mr. Gray chuckled, spitting bits of cookie crumbs as he finished munching down the first sleeve of the wafers. "Dangerous? Yes. Stupid? Extraordinarily so. But not for no reason." Mr. Gray started walking towards the portal without explaining further.

"Ahem." Channie cleared her throat, stopping Mr. Gray in his tracks. "Pray tell, what, then, could possibly be a good reason for saving Jerry?"

Mr. Gray turned around, continuing to walk backwards as he neared the mouth of the portal. "Isn't it obvious?" he asked. "It's friendship. Yours and Stephanie's. The Agares don't value such bonds, but you humans must protect one another if you wish to survive." He gestured behind him towards the portal. "She won't make it back successfully without you. Indulge her. Just stay alert." He vanished through the opening.

Channie sighed. She'd never been all that close with Steph. It still didn't quite feel worth the risk, but she closed her eyes and breathed out all the air from her lungs. Empty lungs eased the transition between worlds. A breath full of air was the fastest way to lose her dinner on the other side. She followed Mr. Gray in.

The air rippled with energy as she passed through the conduit, slipping outside of time entirely. She stepped into the Beyond, feeling the humidity of the air change as if she'd just walked off a plane in Hawaii. She was glad to be able to marvel at the sight of the Parcae's home realm once more. The Beyond was the space between places. The sky overhead swirled with glimmering currents—all the energies of countless universes twisting together and flowing apart simultaneously.

The vast majority of the energy that surrounded her was invisible to the human eye, but the Parcae could read it like a book. Mr. Gray hopped along the barren landscape of dark jagged rocks until he'd found the correct point for reentry into the mortal realm, six years earlier than when they'd left. He opened another portal with another wave of his hand.

Channie wished she could stay a little longer. Being in the Beyond made her feel tiny and insignificant, but in a good way, like looking up at a sky full of stars at night. She imagined this was how astronauts felt when they looked upon the Earth from space. It gave perspective. She didn't want to take her eyes off the shimmering sky, full of such unfettered potential. Few people got to witness such a beautiful sight.

Steph pushed on ahead, stepping into the return portal without looking back. Channie approached the opening and looked down at Mr. Gray. The gluttonous creature was in the process of eating the last wafer cookie. Crumbs tumbled from his chin as he tossed the empty packaging into the portal before realizing that Channie was watching him.

"Didn't want to litter. Best to leave Earth trash on Earth."

Channie followed Mr. Gray back in time. The residual heat of the Beyond vanished in an instant, replaced by the chill of night on Earth in the Pacific Northwest. Tonight, the night Jerry was to be devoured, the sky was ablaze with an aurora borealis display unlike any Channie had ever seen before or since. The sky swirled similarly to the Beyond with surges of color flowing from the north sky. It was beautiful, but anxiety inducing: The unusual display was the result of the Agares and their agents. The charged particles were not coming from the sun, but through weak spots in the universe She was literally witnessing the fires of heaven as the Agares sacked a Parcae stronghold within the Beyond with powerful energy weapons.

Here on Earth around this time, the Agares sent all sorts of terrible creatures from other realms to destroy Channie and her friends. Tonight, it was vampires. They weren't the glittery sort, nor the caped kind. They were called ghasts—winged ghouls that drank blood and lured their victims in with sounds of crying children. Channie had hoped to never be near such terror again.

The ghasts weren't evil—good and evil were human concepts—the creatures simply lived to feed, without moral qualms or empathy. It was their nature.

Steph placed her grocery bags down again. She flexed out her fingers and then squeezed them into a fist repeatedly to shake off the pinch left by the handles digging into her skin.

"You have thirty minutes until the goat gets eaten," said Mr. Gray. "Go to the mess hall and put all that meat into a heavy-duty trash bag. You'll have to make the switch with Jerry quickly to avoid being seen by your past selves."

The portal disintegrated behind them with a crack like thunder. Channie helped Steph gather up the grocery bags. They needed to move quickly in case anyone came to investigate the sound. The bags were heavier than Channie expected, immediately pinching her fingers on both hands, even with only half the load. They hurried towards the mess hall. The strain in her hands made Channie appreciate how hard Steph was working to save Jerry.

They passed several young campers, out and about despite the late hour to watch the unusual northern lights. There were no city lights anywhere nearby to dull the display. No one paid them much mind, probably assuming they were camp counselors. They found the mess hall empty when they arrived.

"Go into the kitchen," said Mr. Gray.

They followed him back around the counter. Mr. Gray pointed at the container of trash bags on the lower shelf as he passed by, continuing on towards a refrigerator that stood against the far wall. Steph placed her grocery bags down on the counter and pulled a trash bag off the roll. Channie placed her bags beside Steph's and immediately got to work emptying out their contents. Butcher-wrapped cuts of goat, some bone in, all needed to be unwrapped and tossed into the trash bag.

A hissing sound startled Channie as she transferred the first cuts. Mr. Gray was spraying a canister of whipped cream into his mouth.

"Hurry," said Steph. "We don't have much time."

Channie returned her attention to the work at hand. Some of the bundles were precut, plastic-wrapped packages, straight from the grocery store aisle. A container of diced up stew meat made Channie raise an eyebrow. Several minutes later, when they were finally done, Channie shined her cellphone's flashlight into the trash bag.

It didn't exactly look like a goat carcass….

The pieces were all perfectly butchered, and there wasn't any hair or blood. Before Channie could say anything, Steph took off her fuzzy white hoodie and threw it into the bag. Mr. Gray held up a couple large bottles of ketchup. The girls each took one and started squeezing.

Pppppppbbbbbbbbbbfffffffffffffhhh.

Steph and Channie both giggled at the gassy sound.

Mr. Gray laughed as well from across the kitchen where he was now both elbows deep into a giant apple crumble. The brown sugar and cinnamon smell was intoxicating, even over the smell of raw meat—time travel was metabolically exhausting. Channie felt the tug of intense cravings on her soul. Her mouth was salivating by the time she finished washing her hands of goat but Steph yanked her away from joining in on the apple crumble with Mr. Gray.

"Focus!" Steph pleaded.

"I know, I know," said Channie. "Jerry is counting on us."

Steph gave a curt nod. Channie helped her heft the garbage bag up over her shoulder.

"Take that broom with you," said Mr. Gray.

Channie snatched up a push broom that was leaning up against the wall by the exit as she passed. "What's this for?" she asked.

Mr. Gray merely smiled. "I'll meet you in the woods once you have the goat."

Channie pursed her lips as Mr. Gray opened a small portal and vanished into the aether. They kept moving, putting distance between themselves and the portal before it popped out of existence. Steph marched ahead, a woman on a mission, refusing to let the goat meat weigh her down.

Channie had forgotten how many campers were out watching the sky before the ghast's impending attack. It was concerning. Danger beyond anything they could imagine was lurking in the woods.

As they passed a group of girls stretched out on a blanket, a not-too-distant scream sent a shiver down Channie's spine. The young campers stopped their chatter at once, sitting up to look towards the treeline. The cry came from the direction Channie and Steph already needed to go.

"Go back to your cabins," ordered Channie. The fear that gripped her came across in her voice. The girls didn't argue, gathering up their blanket without another word.

Channie couldn't be sure, but the scream sounded slightly too high pitched to be human. Steph doubled her pace, forcing Channie to hustle to catch up. Goosebumps appeared on her arms as she scanned her eyes across the dark trees. She couldn't shake the feeling that something was watching her.

Jerry was leashed to a stake outside the last cabin in the line—the one young Steph and Channie had been assigned to. They heard the rattle of the bell that was dangling around Jerry's neck before they saw the goat in the darkness. The inhuman scream had come from the forest beyond.

Too close.

Steph dropped the garbage bag and rushed to Jerry's side. She gripped the goat tightly, as if he were a long-lost brother, burying her face into his neck. "Good boy, Jerry," she said. "I'm here for you now."

Jerry continued with his constant chewing motions, unperturbed as Steph began to unhook his collar. Channie dragged the bag of meat closer, keeping one eye on the sky. Time was short.

Once Steph finished removing Jerry's bell and collar she helped Channie overturn the garbage bag. The pile of meat, ketchup, and Steph's fuzzy hoodie plopped into a ridiculous pile. Channie used the broom to push the pile into a more solid looking lump, draping the hoodie around the outside and tucking the sleeves underneath. At a glance, it was a disturbing sight. She hoped it would fool their younger selves.

Without his leash, Jerry was proving difficult to lead. The goat ignored Steph's urgings and it wasn't until Channie shoved him hard with both hands that he even took a single step.

Mr. Gray had said to meet them in the woods, but that was also where the ghasts were hiding. Nevertheless, Channie and Steph continued to push and pull on Jerry, urging him closer to the treeline.

A blood-curdling scream pierced the night. It sounded like a child being ripped limb from limb, but Channie and Steph knew better. They craned their necks up just in time to see a dark shape dart by overhead. A ghast, about the size of a large dog, landed on top of the meat pile. Jerry's bell jingled as the ghast slashed at the hoodie with razor sharp talons. It soon realized the deception, however. The creature emitted a series of low clicks that almost sounded like a growl.

"*Meh-eh-eh!*" bleated Jerry. He no longer required urging to move.

The ghast spun towards Jerry and the girls, crying out a breathy sob with the voice of a young child. Jerry ran ahead, leaving Steph and Channie to sprint after him. A swoosh sounded as the ghast spread its wings wide once more and took flight. Channie stumbled over her own feet as she struggled to chase after Jerry. She had to keep looking over her shoulder in order to stay aware of the ghast's position at the same time. They managed to reach the treeline before the ghast could land an attack. It thudded back to the ground at the edge of the forest.

Jerry continued to dash ahead, leaving the girls behind as the ghast scurried up the nearest tree and began hopping between the upper foliage. It was stalking them. The ghast made no attempt to hide its position, mocking them with continued sobs that raised the hairs on the backs of their necks.

With a piercing screech, the ghast finally made its attack, lunging down at Channie. She steeled her grip on the broom handle, spinning in place to face the terrible creature. She swung the push broom like she was aiming at a piñata. The ghast hooked its claws into the bristles, tearing the head clean off the broom and sending the broken handle flying free of Channie's grasp. She fell backwards into the dirt. The attack was deflected, but Channie was left defenseless.

The ghast tucked its wings against its sides as it turned to face her once more. It paused, opening up its snout of jagged teeth, but instead of growling or crying out again it merely laughed—a child's giggle.

Channie felt around behind her for the broom handle, but found nothing but dirt and tree roots. The ghast continued to laugh as it rushed in on her with a multitude of short steps.

Steph jumped out from behind a tree, the broken broom handle held up above her head like a spear. The laughter caught in the ghasts throat as Steph staked the broom handle straight through its chest.

The ghast stared up at her with its jowls hanging open. It collapsed over on its side, chuckling one last time before succumbing to the fatal wound.

"*Meh-eh-eh*," bleated Jerry, standing obediently by Steph's side.

Steph rubbed the goat's head absentmindedly as she looked upon Channie. "Close one," she said.

Before Channie could even take another breath, another child-like chuckle rang out from above in the trees, followed by a third and a forth, until it sounded like an entire kindergarten class was chattering above their heads.

"Hurry!" cried the high-pitched voice of Mr. Gray.

Channie searched her surroundings until she found the lone Parcae off to her left beside the hazy patch of another portal.

Steph slapped Jerry's haunch, sending the animal in the right direction. Channie scrambled to follow behind Steph as she dove for the portal. The child-like laughter shifted into an uproar of screams as the ghasts saw what was happening. Channie lunged into the portal without looking back.

She landed on her chest with a thud in the Beyond. The flat stone shards that made up the walkway she was on jangled against one another as she turned over to look behind her. Mr. Gray reached up and ripped the corners of the portal down with his hands, eyes wide with a genuine look of fear that Channie had never before seen on his tiny face.

"Circumstances have changed…" he said with surprise in his voice. "There usually aren't so many of them there. Excuse me, I need to change my pants."

Beside her, Steph and Jerry were both retching out the contents of their stomachs. Neither had exhaled before rushing through the portal. Channie hadn't remembered to breathe out either, but her reflex had become to breathe out at a portal surface just as one automatically holds their breath as they jump into a pool.

Channie had never seen a goat projectile vomit before.

"You okay, Hun?" she asked Steph.

The resilient girl gave a thumbs up as she heaved once more into the pile in front of her.

Jerry finished barfing and immediately began eating it again. Channie gagged and turned away. She had her limits.

Mr. Gray opened a final portal for them to return home. "See you next time," he said. Steph, looking more pale than usual, gave him one last hug before directing Jerry through the opening.

"I wouldn't mind if you left me out of the next adventure," said Channie.

Mr. Gray chuckled boisterously. "Now what would be the fun in that?"

Channie gave him a one finger salute as she prepared to step through what she knew would not be her final portal, despite her protests.

Mr. Gray blew her a kiss.

"You better not be the death of me," she muttered as she left the Beyond once more.

When she emerged on the other side, Jerry was already in the process of barfing again.

"Thank you," said Steph. "I honestly don't know what I would have done without you. I can never thank you enough…."

"Don't mention it," said Channie.

"No, really," Steph insisted. "Jerry was my dad's last present to me before he passed away earlier that summer. This means the world to me."

Channie's eyes immediately welled up with tears.

"No, no, don't cry," said Steph. "That was a long time ago."

Channie buried her face in Steph's hair, grabbing her in a tight hug. After a moment, Steph clung back onto her just as desperately. Neither one pulled away until they were both sniffling.

"I want pie," Steph pouted through her tears.

Channie could have cried again, this time with pure joy.

"There's a diner down the street," she said. "I'll buy."

"Can we get one of every kind?" asked Steph.

"Of course!" laughed Channie.

The Tall Man

Josie and Rebecca stayed just within the treeline as they walked.

"I can't believe you did that!" exclaimed Rebecca. "You're probably going to get sent home, but that was the most badass thing I've ever seen."

Josie blushed slightly, feeling awkward. She wasn't used to compliments. In hindsight, pulling a knife on Steph probably hadn't been the best idea. By now Steph had probably told Matt exactly where his missing knife ended up. Josie figured her camp experience would be coming to a premature end as soon as one of the counselors found her.

Rebecca looked thoughtful for a moment. "If you ditch the knife, I'll just tell everyone Steph is lying," she said.

It was a nice gesture, but Josie knew it would be impossible for her not to look guilty. She also wasn't about to throw away her protection—not while she was still uncertain about the tall man.

"You *are* going to throw away the knife, right?" asked Rebecca.

Josie stepped over a root. It had been her plan from the start to search through the woods today. "Yeah, sure, of course." *Once I'm sure I'm safe.*

They were nearing the girls' cabins and the section of woods where she'd seen the slender figure standing. The peach-fuzz hairs on her neck and arms stood up at the mere thought of being so close to where the figure had been perched. Up ahead, an impression in the topsoil drew Josie in.

She raced over to the soft dirt and squatted down beside the impression. She could make out two distinct footprints, each about a foot and a half long, placed side-by-side, facing the cabins. She scoured the forest floor for more prints and found there to be a distinct trail leading back, deeper into the woods.

"Do you know what this means?" asked Josie, leaning in closer to the pair of prints beside her.

"You found Bigfoot!" exclaimed Rebecca, laughing hysterically.

Josie glared up at her. "No. Well, maybe. But what I'm trying to say is, this proves something really was out here this morning."

Rebecca rolled her eyes. "I told you, this must just be a prank by the boys." She hopped along from one footprint to the next. "'Ooow, Bigfoot's in the woods!'" she said mockingly. "How cliché. Tomorrow it'll be the Loch Ness Monster down by the boathouse."

"I'm serious," said Josie. "You see the stride it had. And not even a professional basketball player has feet this big."

Rebecca continued to hop along. She was barely able to make the leaps. "I saw a documentary about Bigfoot last year. People were just using wooden cut-outs to make the prints. Pressing them into the ground and jumping on them to make trails. It's exactly the kind of stupid stuff boys like to do."

Looking closely at the impressions, Josie could make out several toe divots. It was as if the creature was curling its toes under while it stood, digging them deeper into the earth. One clear toe divot even showed a groove, possibly from some sort of thick, pointed nail or claw. She clutched the knife at her side a little bit harder.

"The boys definitely did not make these," she said as she ran her finger along the claw slice. The ground was hard to the touch. It must have taken a lot of pressure to form the mark.

Rebecca didn't respond.

Josie looked up. "Rebecca?" she called, a little bit louder.

Still nothing.

She stood up and started walking deeper into the woods in the direction of the prints. "Rebecca!" she called out again. An anxious knot formed in her stomach. "This isn't funny! Come out now!"

Rebecca was gone.

Her gut told her she needed to get out of there—to head back to camp where there were other people, where it was safer, but she couldn't leave Rebecca out here alone. She picked up her pace, jogging between the trees.

"Rebecca! Where are you?" she cried.

Branches whipped against her as she dashed ahead. The trail of impressions continued. Worry rose inside of her with every step.

God dammit, Rebecca!

A twig snapped in the near distance catching her attention. She stopped and turned her head to face the sound. She was about to call out again when—

Thud.

A sound reminiscent of a heavy stone being dropped to the dirt filled her with extra caution. A moment later—

Thud.

The second clomp sent a shiver down Josie's spine.

Thud. Thud.

Lumbering footsteps—something sizable was moving nearby. She ducked down behind a thick tree trunk, immediately regretting her decision to investigate the woods in the first place.

Thud. Thud. Thud. Thud.

It was getting closer. Josie felt like a rabbit hiding from a coyote. A pressure was building inside of her—energy deep in her muscles. She had to make a run for it. She'd been on the track team in seventh grade, but the uneven surface of the forest floor was not an ideal course. She took off at a sprint anyway, back in the direction of the cabins.

The thuds stopped for a short moment when she began running, but then picked up pace, honing in on her footfalls.

Thud, thud, thud, thud, thud.

Leaves rustled and branches snapped as whatever was behind her mounted a pursuit.

Josie nearly turned her ankle on a root but continued running as fast as her feet would carry her.

Thud thud thud. Thud thud thud.

The pace changed—suddenly sounding more like a galloping horse.

Josie burst through the treeline and ran directly into an older boy. They both tumbled to the ground. The boy grunted in pain as he landed sprawled out in the grassy clearing.

Josie took the fall hard. The wind was knocked out of her. She gasped for air, unable to take a full breath. The panic in her chest made her feel ready to burst. The boy was first to get back to his feet. Josie grasped onto the grass with her fingers and forced her body back up into a kneeling position.

"Are you alright?" asked the boy, concern etched into his brow.

Josie slowly regained her breath. Her chest was still heaving hard, leaving her unable to piece together any words as she scanned her eyes back and forth across the dense woods. She listened intently, but the thuds had ceased.

The boy offered her his hand, helping her climb back up onto her feet. His palm was hot to the touch as his fingers interlocked with her own. His hand stayed clutched to hers for a lingering moment after she was already standing and steady.

Josie narrowed her eyes as she took in the boy's appearance. He had a dark red spattering across the front of his faded blue hoodie, which looked an awful lot like blood.

"It's paint," he said upon taking in her concerned expression. *That was a lie.*

Josie looked back into the woods, searching for anything out of place.

Only trees and dirt....

"What are you running from?" the boy asked, matching her serious demeanor.

Josie wasn't sure what to say. She didn't want to sound crazy, but Rebecca was still out there somewhere. "I don't know," she said truthfully between gasps for air. "There was something big. We were following some tracks."

The boy's eyes grew wide.

"Maybe a bear," she added. The lie was the only way she could think of to be taken seriously.

The boy turned towards the woods while pulling up his right sleeve. He had some sort of strange silver bracelet coiled around his wrist and forearm.

"You said 'we'?" he asked. "Is someone still out there?"

Josie nodded frantically. "My friend, Rebecca."

"Go back to your cabin," he said.

Josie stared at him oddly.

"Now!" he ordered before running headlong into the woods, leaving Josie with her mouth hanging open.

Now we're rolling along at full steam! I do love so very much watching our little chess pieces dance around with one another. It is sad to say that Rebecca's fate is a complete toss-up at this point... it's difficult to see where everything will land with all of this other-worldly attention raining down upon the campground and nearby woods tonight. I've seen this night play out both ways for poor little Rebecca....

Keep vigilant,

-Mr. Gray

Terrifying Truth

Josie didn't wait around to see what would happen to the strange boy. Anyone who would run headlong into the woods after being told there was a *bear* nearby wasn't right in the head. At some point bravery was more aptly called stupidity.

He must be deranged... she mused.

She sprinted back past the line of girls' cabins, quickly passing her own cabin. She wasn't about to let anyone else tell her where to hide. She didn't trust the blood-splattered white boy.

What was he even doing over here?

Boys had no business on the girls' side of camp. He was too young to be a counselor.

A kernel of doubt crept into her mind.

Could Rebecca have been right?

Before disappearing, Rebecca had been convinced all the oddities in the woods were just the boys pranking them... before she disappeared.

Josie's self-preservation instinct overcame her skepticism. Most people couldn't see danger until it poked them in the eye. Josie knew the terrifying truth. The dark depths of the universe held monsters far worse than those depicted at the edges of ancient maps. Today, she could feel the malicious energy exuding from the forest.

Josie looked back again when she reached the last cabin in the line. The trees stood silent—no breeze to rustle their branches. There was no sign of Rebecca, the boy, or anything else. Josie didn't know what she'd seen, but she certainly knew what she felt. The fine hairs on the backs of her arms were all still standing up tall. There was an electric charge lingering in the air above. It fell upon the campground like a static snowfall, every stray current reminding Josie to be mindful.

She spotted Matt Greene skulking around the counselors' offices. Chances were Steph had already told him who stole his belt knife. Josie made a beeline towards a group of girls in the distance that were setting up easels in preparation for an art class. She wanted to stay in a public place around as many people as possible while also avoiding Matt.

She grabbed an easel and set of art supplies and sat quietly in the back of the pack facing the distant woods. Worry for Rebecca outweighed everything else on her mind. She considered going to the counselors for help despite her likely expulsion from the camp, especially as morning dipped into afternoon, but she knew from past experience that merely talking seriously about supernatural occurrences was the fastest way to end up locked up in a mental institute. She would need proof before anyone would listen to a word of her story.

She dipped her brush mindlessly in a mixture of greens and browns she'd lined up on her palette.

"What is *that*?" asked the counselor leading the activity. She was standing over Josie's shoulder.

Josie glanced back, not realizing at first that the woman was asking about the painting.

"That's super creepy," she said.

Josie looked back over at her easel. A rough painting of the forest included the tall figure she'd seen that morning. Her imagination had filled in more detail than her eyes had been capable of observing.

"Oh," said Josie. "I'm sorry." She didn't know what else to say.

The counselor's face remained pinched up with distaste as she moved on to the next camper.

As soon as the counselor looked away Josie ran the thickest brush she had through a dollop of black paint and blotted out the eerie figure, slender limbs and all. The gesture did nothing to alleviate the feeling that the forest was still watching her.

In the distance, a normal-sized figure emerged from the treeline. The baby blue of the boy's hoodie gave him away. He moved with purpose in his steps, making a beeline for Josie's cabin. He went inside for a moment before popping back out again with a frustrated look on his face. The cabin was probably empty this time of day.

How did he know which one was mine?

The boy must have been watching her prior to their run-in. If she hadn't felt sketched out by him before, she certainly did now. He stood outside the cabin's entrance scanning his eyes across the campground until they landed on the art class. He started moving in her direction.

Shoot.

She hadn't been as clever as she thought. If she stayed put he would find her quickly, but if she ran now, she would have a little bit of a lead. She dropped her brush and put all of her pent-up anxiety to good use, sprinting out of the art class and away from the boy. She didn't look back, instead simply assuming that the boy was hot on her trail.

Her mind raced to come up with somewhere to hide, but the open grassy fields of the campground didn't supply any cover. She had no idea where she was going to go until her frantic gaze fell across Channie, sitting by herself at the end of the kayak dock. She looked to be zoning out, taking in the scenic view.

If there was a day for unsupervised water sports, it was today. Josie changed her direction, sprinting downhill towards the water's edge. The Puget Sound shimmered in the sunlight as the breezy afternoon winds stirred up the gray sea water into a choppy slosh that was less-than optimal for kayaking.

She hit the head of the dock at full speed, her feet slapping hard against the slightly uneven wooden planks. Channie looked up at the sound, a concerned expression already nestled upon her brow. Josie didn't stop running until she reached her. Channie's attention shifted behind Josie.

Josie glanced back for the first time since she began her sprint. The boy was indeed chasing after her, and he had closed in on her lead vastly.

"Kayak," Josie gasped, out of breath.

Channie was already on her feet. The girls quickly lifted a two-person kayak from one of the stands on the side of the dock and plopped it down on the water. Josie grabbed a pair of paddles from a large bucket, and then shoved the whole container holding the rest of them over the side of the dock. The girls stepped gingerly into the kayak, nearly flipping it over in their haste.

The slap of the boy's feet sounded on the dock as they pushed off. The boy came to a stop at the end of the dock, leaning against his own thighs as he panted for air.

Josie and Channie paddled vigorously, putting as much distance as they could between themselves and the strangely determined boy.

Josie is rightly being cautious about the boy, but she isn't seeing the whole picture yet. It is good to see Channie's thread entangling with Josie's though! Neither one of them has any inkling of the importance of their friendship yet. A beautiful tapestry. It's funny how easily both of their lives could have gone any number of seemingly infinite different ways, and yet here they both are. Remember, only one path escapes ultimate disaster, and it's going to take a whole lot of pieces falling into place to get there.

Keep vigilant,

-Mr. Gray

CHAPTER

6

Dark Water

The kayak rolled across the choppy waters with a slight bounce as the waves slapped against the narrow hull. The girls didn't stop paddling until they were about fifty yards out from the dock. The boy remained at the end of the dock, watching as they floated aimlessly with nowhere to go.

Channie was in the front seat. She turned her upper body around to look at Josie questioningly.

Josie took a deep breath. "That thing we saw this morning was real," she said. "I went into the forest with Rebecca. Something is out there. I don't know where Rebecca is. She just vanished."

"You left her out there?"

Josie frowned. "She left me! But we really should try to find her."

"We?" Channie asked, incredulously.

Josie looked to her pleadingly. "I can't exactly go to the counselors with this."

"No one would believe any of it," Channie agreed. "So what's with the *guy*?" Channie asked, gesturing with her paddle towards the older boy, still skulking at them from the end of the dock. He was sitting down now, his legs dangling just above the water.

The way he looked at her put a nervous pit in Josie's stomach. It wasn't that she was afraid of him. She had a knife and was more than capable of defending herself. She was not weak, nor stupid. But still, the pained expression on his face held something that disturbed her. He was looking at her like he knew her.

You don't know me.

She narrowed her eyes at him disapprovingly across the water. "I don't know who he is, but he's been following me," said Josie.

The longer they waited offshore, the more concerned Josie became with the boy's willpower. They paddled around for what must have been hours, but the boy never moved from his spot on the dock.

"He isn't going to quit," said Channie, exasperated and bored out of her mind. "Let's just head back in and beat him up. We can probably take him together. He looks kind of scrawny." She wasn't joking.

Josie pursed her lips. She was inclined to agree. The sun was starting to get low and she felt exhausted. Her legs were cramped up from sitting in the kayak all day.

Before she could respond, a stroke of luck landed in their favor: Matt Greene came strutting down the dock and immediate began yelling at the boy about the submerged bucket of paddles.

Josie and Channie didn't squander the distraction. They paddled hard with the slight current, moving down the shoreline and then in towards the rocky beach. The ominous forest stood just beyond the edge of the water.

Josie stopped paddling as the sound of a large splash farther down the shore drew her attention. The water was rippling wildly, as if a cannonball had just touched down.

Channie stopped paddling as well. A moment later, something bumped the bottom of the kayak violently. Both girls braced themselves, trying to steady the rocking.

"I think I saw a fin!" said Channie. "Did a shark just ram us?"

Josie searched the dark water. It was difficult to see anything through the glare of the low sun.

Thud! Another bump sent the kayak rolling dangerously to one side.

Josie saw something too, this time. It was the size of a large dog, gliding through the water with ease. What Channie thought was a fin looked more like a giant bat wing to Josie— hairy and veiny, and about three feet long.

That's not *a shark....*

They paddled harder as whatever it was made one last pass, ramming the front corner of the kayak. It stopped them as abruptly as hitting a rock and jarred the hull sideways, parallel to the shoreline.

Channie screamed. She drew her kayak paddle from the water and gripped it by one end. She swung it down over her head like an axe, slapping the water ineffectively. After several more swings, the paddle was yanked from her hands and disappeared under the surface of the water for good.

Josie drew her paddle through the water more shallowly, afraid of what might happen if she lost hers as well. They needed to get back to the shore, and quickly!

Another splash sounded in the distance, followed by a strange chittering coming from the forest that didn't sound like any bird Josie had ever heard before. She focused on working her paddle efficiently, though her heart was racing faster than ever before.

The chitters grew higher in pitch until it morphed into a child-like giggle.

"Oh, hell no!" exclaimed Channie.

As soon as they reached shallow enough water, Channie and Josie both flopped out of the kayak and high-stepped their way through the surf. The loose rocks on the beach clinked together as they sprinted down the shoreline, back towards the campground. They didn't stop running until the abandoned kayak was out of sight and their stiff legs had turned to jelly. Wet socks squished in their shoes uncomfortably as they continued back towards their cabin at a slow jog, breathing hard.

Neither Matt, nor the odd boy was anywhere to be seen as they skirted past the dock. They hardly seemed threatening anymore by contrast. People could be reasoned with— monsters, not so much.

Channie remained ahead of Josie, her wide-eyed stare focused on their destination. When they reached the row of cabins, they found some of the other girls setting up blankets on the grass, gazing up towards the dimming sky. Steph was among them. She shot Josie a dark glower as she passed.

Once inside the cabin, Channie immediately began throwing all of her belongings into her suitcase.

"We still need to search for Rebecca," Josie reminded her. She slipped off her wet shoes and dumped atleast an ounce of water out of each of them.

"Yeah, I'm not doing that," said Channie. She didn't even glance up from her frantic packing. "That wasn't natural."

Josie frowned. She wasn't any more pleased with the prospect of looking for Rebecca than Channie was, but she felt obligated. "The last ferry already left for the night," she said. "There's no way off the island until morning."

"Then I'm leaving first thing in the morning," said Channie. She sat down on the edge of her bunk and kicked off her wet shoes. She buried her face in her hands, leaning against her knees with her elbows.

Their twenty-year-old cabin leader, Alison Cartwright, poked her head in through the door and called out to them: "You girls won't want to miss this!" she exclaimed. "The northern lights are visible. Like, *really* visible!" She disappeared back out through the door.

Channie lifted her head up. "That's some bad omen crap," she said. "I swear to god, if those things eat me first…."

Despite her protests, Channie followed Josie's lead, putting on dry shoes and grabbing flashlights before exiting the cabin.

Outside, despite the sky not being all the way dark yet, the aurora borealis was shimmering with a grand display.

Everyone was lying down, staring up at the dancing lights as they flashed with a golden hue.

"It looks like the sky's on fire," said Steph, her eyes wide with awe.

In stoic silence, Josie and Channie slinked away from the viewing party. Josie clutched Matt's knife tightly in her fist inside her pocket. The forest loomed in the near distance.

With everyone else's eyes locked on the sky, Josie kept hers aimed lower. The terrors kept to the fringes no longer. The shadows had malicious intent.

It is not the sky that is burning.... This is a sad phase for my species. The Agares lay waste to our city in the Beyond. It is our punishment for meddling in the lives of the humans. The pendulum swings freely, and so now it is my time to stay vigilant.

Best wishes,

-Mr. Gray

CHAPTER

7

Jerry (the goat)

Their cabin was the last one in the line. As they rounded the edge of the structure, the clang of a bell made both girls jump.

"*Meh-eh-eh.*"

Jerry, the goat, was tied to a stake. The bell around his neck jingled again as he turned to watch them pass with his soulless eyes.

"Freaking goat," said Channie.

Jerry chewed mindlessly on a clump of grass.

"Come on," said Josie. "It will be fully dark soon. I don't want to spend a minute longer out here than we need to."

The forest remained silent as they reached the edge of the treeline. Channie's flashlight flickered slightly and dimmed. She bashed it firmly against the palm of her hand, jarring the batteries around with a clunky rattle. "I swear…."

Josie pulled the belt knife out of her pocket and unsheathed it from its leather holster as they stepped into the woods. She held it down at her side, pointed away from her to avoid any accidents. After everything she had seen she wanted to be fully prepared for anything.

Channie wasn't surprised by the blade, having watched Josie steal it that morning. Josie, on the other hand, was taken off guard when Channie pulled out a knife of her own—a butterfly knife with a black grip. Josie gawked at her as she flourished the blade into its ready position with a flick of her wrist.

"You should always be prepared when going into the woods," said Channie.

Channie was a practical girl.

Once again starting from the spot where they'd seen the tall figure that morning, Josie led Channie roughly along the path she'd taken with Rebecca.

"Should we call out for her?" Channie whispered. "Or nah…?"

Josie contemplated the ramifications. It felt unwise. She shook her head. The shadows of the trees felt oppressive. Anything could be lurking behind any of the trunks. The beams of their flashlights made the shadows shift. The dark voids seemed dense until the light jumped across them as the girls scanned back and forth along the trail of prints. They could only see a dozen or so yards ahead through the brush.

Channie stopped beside one of the deeper footprint impressions in the soil. Her resolve to continue their search visibly waned as her face drooped. She placed her own foot, tiny in comparison, within the large footprint. "He'd need some massive sneakers," she whispered.

Josie chose not to mention the nail grooves she'd taken note of earlier. She could tell Channie was already scared enough.

The last glimmers of daylight drained from the sky as they continued deeper into the woods. Josie had hoped to have more time before full dark. As they followed the footprints farther than Josie had traveled with Rebecca, Josie felt tension rising in her chest. She nearly plowed into the back of Channie as the girl made a sudden stop.

Before Josie could say anything, Channie aimed her flashlight on a divergent path, off to the left. A second trail of equally large footprints crossed the first. Either whatever-it-was was walking around all over the place, or there was more than one.

"Which way should we go?" asked Channie.

A male voice spoke out from behind Josie. "How about straight back where you came from."

Both girls spun around on the spot, their hearts jumping into their throats. They hadn't noticed the older boy from the dock trailing after them.

Josie sprang at him with her knife held high.

"Ahh!" the boy shrieked as he stumbled backwards over a fallen log.

Josie jumped on top of him in an instant and held her knife up to his throat.

"Where's Rebecca?" she demanded.

Channie stepped up beside them and posed threateningly with one hand on her hip.

The boy's expression shifted from surprised to amused. A thin smile cracked his lips, which then quickly turned into a full on grin.

"What's so funny?" Josie asked. She lifted herself up slightly and then slammed her butt back down hard into the boy's stomach.

He grunted.

"I don't know where your friend is!" he insisted.

Josie squeezed his ribs with her knees. "Why are you stalking me?"

He grunted again at the rib jab. "Oof! Quit that! I'm not stalking you, I'm just trying to keep you safe! There are things out here in the woods that you should do your best to avoid...."

Channie flourished her butterfly knife as she dropped down beside the boy's head. She pressed her blade menacingly against the other side of his throat. "Like pervy boys?" she asked. "Are you a pervert??" She had a crazed look in her eyes.

The boy's eyebrows drooped, worry returning to his face. "No! Of course not! My name is Lewis, and I was sent here to protect you, Josie." Lewis's cheeks went flush.

Josie felt her own face grow hot as well. She eased off, withdrawing her knife slightly. "Who sent you?" she asked.

A distant scream tore through the underbrush. The cry came from deeper in the forest. Something was unusual about the pitch of the scream.... It sounded slightly too high to be human. There was something animalistic about it.

"That wasn't Rebecca..." said Channie.

That wasn't human....

"We should go," said Lewis.

Josie scrambled back up to her feet. She extended her hand to help Lewis up as well. He accepted it, but grabbed on awkwardly with his left hand instead of his right. Around his right wrist and forearm the strange silver bracelet-thingy Josie noticed earlier was spiraled around, looking like an odd piece of ancient Egyptian jewelry. Josie had never seen anything like it before. Lewis kept his arm held stiff with his hand closed, as if protecting it.

Channie's face remained frozen in a frown as she stared off in the direction of the unnerving scream, eyes locked on the darkness. Josie pulled her along, following after Lewis as he retraced their steps.

Lewis didn't have a flashlight with him. He must have been relying on their light the whole way in. He set a quick pace now, moving at a medium jog. They had to dodge trees and block branches with their arms to stop from being whipped in the face.

A cackling giggle that sounded like a ticklish young child rang out from somewhere behind and up above. It was as if something was trying to lure them back. The thought filled Josie with dread.

The edge of the forest came upon them suddenly. They burst through the treeline, but then Lewis stopped and put his arms out, ushering them back within the shadows.

"Turn off the lights!" he whispered harshly.

A blood-curdling scream pierced the night, coming from directly above them. A dark shape glided overhead in the clearing between them and the line of cabins. She could make out bat-like wings, the same as the creature that bumped their kayak. It was skinny with gangly limbs that looked almost reptilian in nature as they dangled beneath it. It was difficult to make out anything more in the dark, but one thing Josie knew for certain was that it was bigger than she was. It was not from this world.

She ducked behind the last row of trees with Lewis and Channie.

The creature swooped down, landing with a thud on top of Jerry the goat. His bell jingled as the creature slashed and bit at him viciously. There was no movement from the goat when the creature was finished with its attack. It snapped its jaws quickly like a bird, picking apart its tethered prey.

The terror emitted a series of low clicks that almost sounded like a growl as it looked around. *"Ooow wooh waah!"* it cried out, vocalizing a breathy sob in the voice of a young child.

A moment later, it launched itself back up into the air and disappeared from sight. The whole attack lasted less than twenty seconds start to finish.

That garbage bag full of ketchup and meat somehow did the trick! None of the kids were any the wiser. Now Jerry is a lot like Schrödinger's cat, alive and dead at the same time, depending on your perspective! I love little tricks like this! It keeps so many fresh elements in play for us to use in the war against the Agares! They can't keep track of all the shuffling pieces... but I can!

Keep vigilant,

-Mr. Gray

CHAPTER

8

The Untimely Demise of Annabel Wence

The creature wasn't even gone ten seconds before camp counselors Matt and Alison came running around the corner of the cabin to investigate its cries. The beams of their flashlights bounced wildly as they hurried. They'd been watching the unusual aurora borealis together beneath a blanket on the opposite side of the cabin from where all the girls were set up.

Their lights fell across Jerry, the state of which made Alison audibly gasp.

"There must be a bobcat!" exclaimed Matt, scanning the area around them with his flashlight. "We need to get everyone inside!"

Josie, Channie, and Lewis sprinted from the edge of the woods, mixing with the group of stargazing girls just as Alison and Matt announced a lockdown. Lewis was ushered into Josie and Channie's cabin along with all the girls. The counselors left them unsupervised as they continued down the line of

58

cabins, sending everyone they found wandering the grounds inside the buildings nearest to them.

"Why is there a boy in our cabin?" asked Steph, gawking at Lewis.

The whole cabin, abuzz with nervous energy, suddenly fell silent, all eyes turning towards the lone boy.

"He's here so he doesn't get eaten by the bobcat," said Josie, sticking with the terrestrial explanation.

Steph's expression changed as she comprehended the danger. "Jerry's still outside!" she exclaimed.

Josie and Channie looked at each other. Neither one of them wanted to tell Steph of Jerry's demise.

Steph started towards the door but Lewis stopped her. "No one's going out there," he said. "It's not safe tonight."

Steph looked Lewis up and down with a slow pan of her head. Her expression changed again as she submitted to his authority. Without skipping a beat, she fluttered her eyelashes at him in a flirtatious manner.

Josie felt a spike of annoyance which only grew stronger as Steph gestured towards Rebecca's empty bunk.

"My bunkmate didn't make it back for the night," said Steph. "You can take her bed."

Lewis ignored the offer, walking straight over to Josie instead. "I told you, I need to watch over you," he said. He sat down on the bunk beside Josie's, displacing Mia, the girl who belonged there, over to Rebecca's bunk.

Mia didn't complain but she did send Josie a wide-eyed, knowing glance as she walked away.

Josie felt her face go flush again. The small aisle separating her from Lewis may as well have not existed from the looks she received from the rest of the girls as she ventured a quick scan of the cabin.

"I'll keep you safe," said Lewis. "Get some rest."

The embarrassment coursing through Josie's veins was palpable. She lay back on her pillow and closed her eyes despite knowing full well she wouldn't be getting any sleep. She could feel Lewis's eyes on her, even through her eyelids. She didn't understand why he was so fixated on her. She didn't think she was anything special, not in this camp full of girls anyway, many of which she felt were more attractive and developed than she was.

Josie's cheeks warmed. She peaked at Lewis with one eye and caught his gaze lingering across her body. He shifted his eyes back up to her face in an instant. Her cheeks grew even hotter.

She turned to face the wall. His gaze made her feel insecure. He looked at her so intensely. She could still feel the eyes on her back, but the longer she sat with the feeling the more comforting it became instead of intrusive. He still looked at her like he knew her… it was so strange.

"Y'all aren't really trying to go to sleep right now, are you?" Steph complained to the whole cabin. "It's a spooky night. We should be telling ghost stories!"

Some of the other girls were enthusiastic about the idea. Several of them moved closer, sitting on the bunks around Steph as she jumped straight into a story. She always had to be the center of attention.

"Once there was a girl named Annabel Wence. She attended this camp until one night, five summers ago, when her body was found floating face down under the kayak dock!" Steph gestured broadly for dramatic effect. The other girls giggled. "You won't find it funny to learn that her spirit haunts these grounds to this very day, terrorizing anyone unfortunate enough to come across her. She is searching for the ones responsible for her death, for you see, when they found her, there was no water in her lungs—it was not an accident! Annabel was already dead when her body was thrown in! Now, who among you would like to learn of the untimely demise of poor Annabel Wence?"

Other than Channie, who rolled her eyes, all the other girls were feeding right out of Steph's hands.

"Annabel started out her final day at camp just like any other, attending breakfast in the mess hall. She ate alone—not unusual for Annabel—but the kids who saw her that morning noticed something very wrong. Her forehead, beneath her bangs, bore an ashy mark that looked like someone had put a cigar out on it, but she didn't seem to notice it at all. What Annabel didn't know was that she'd been marked to be taken!"

Outside the cabin, there was a sudden onset of heavy rain. A gust of wind struck the side of the building, blowing raindrops against the window. Mia jumped, startled by the sound. The rest of the girls laughed, cutting the tension. It was unusual weather for an unusual night. A late summer storm was blowing in from the north, chilling the air.

"Annabel needed to be careful, but she didn't know how much danger she was in. None of the campers who saw her told her about the mark on her head. Her spirit still blames the kids for not warning her. After breakfast, she decided to take a shortcut through the forest to her first activity of the day, but she never arrived. Eventually, search parties were sent out to find her when she didn't return. It was three full weeks later when her body finally turned up. She looked as fresh as if she had died that very day.

A drifter was found, living illegally in a tent within the edge of the campgrounds. The police arrested him under suspicion of Annabel's murder. He insisted he was innocent right up until the day the state ended his life with lethal injection. His story never changed. He claimed to have heard the howls of a beast the night before Annabel went missing—the very devil himself—and a deep voice had spoken to him inside his head, telling him not to watch as the demon came that would take Annabel."

Another gust of wind whistled in the rafters of the old cabin. A distant crack of thunder punctuated the story.

"But the drifter didn't do as the voice commanded. He saw what came for Annabel, and he tried to stop it! From the shadows it formed, forked-tongued and horned. The drifter was petrified with fear as the shadow crawled up to him and entered his skin. He was no longer in control of his own body.

The beast in human skin waited in the forest for Annabel to pass. He stood perfectly still, not wanting to startle her too soon. When he snatched her, she couldn't even muster a scream as he dragged her away to some underground lair for three weeks of torture."

"What did he do to her?" asked Mia.

"Don't interrupt!" exclaimed Steph. "You don't even want to know what he did. It was too terrible to speak of. Now, Annabel haunts and kills anyone who dares sleep in her old bunk. Which just so happens to be in this very cabin… right there!" Steph pointed at Mia, in Rebecca's bed, just as the door to the cabin burst open.

Everyone screamed—Mia shrieked exceptionally loud. They all turned towards the door. A dark mess of stringy black hair leaned in through the opening. Josie was on her feet in an instant.

Rebecca!

A diluted smear of blood decorated her shirt. Josie ran across the cabin to her as she stumbled in. Her clothing was completely saturated with rain and she had scrapes and scratches up and down her body.

"Help me," Rebecca rasped as she fell into Josie's arms.

Rebecca's still kicking! That's good for my plan. You'll just have to wait around and see how it all unfolds. If I told you now, it would take all the fun away! I hope Steph's little story didn't scare you too much. She made it up completely on the fly. It's a little bit ironic that Annabel's story is that of a marked girl fighting terrors beyond her control, since that is so similar to Steph's own true fate. She does not know it yet, and would dread it if she did, but even Steph has a role to play in the war to come.

Keep vigilant,
-Mr. Gray

CHAPTER

9

Night Terrors

Lewis rushed to help Josie with Rebecca. They each took an arm and helped maneuver her to the nearest bunk to lie down. Rebecca was not in good shape—it looked like she'd rolled through a patch of blackberry brambles, except the cuts were deeper. Her scalp had an abrasion and was bleeding down her face and neck. Her eyes were unfocused, staring off into the distance and her expression remained blank, even as the rest of the cabin erupted in a ruckus.

"The bobcat got her…" said Steph, eyes wide with terror.

Josie knew better.

"Everyone stay back—give her some space," said Lewis.

Channie came closer as everyone else crowded to the back of the cabin. "We need to get the hell out of this camp," she said.

Rebecca grabbed ahold of the front of Josie's shirt and pulled her down until they were face to face. "Flying monsters…" she rasped in a whisper. "They took me to their den and fed on

64

my blood...." She was looking pale from more than just the cold. "I didn't think I was going to make it back."

Josie clasped Rebecca's face with her hands as the girl broke down into tears. "It's okay," she said, "you're back now." Rebecca grasped onto her in a tight hug as she whimpered.

"We're not out of the woods yet," said Lewis. "Your friend is right—we need to get off this island."

"There's no more ferries until morning," said Channie.

"Then we need to be on the first one out," said Lewis. "How far do you think the ferry dock is from here by foot?"

"By foot!?" Channie shook her head, "It's on the other side of the island. It would take hours."

"Then we better get moving," said Lewis. "If we stay, we're dead by morning."

Rebecca sat up abruptly. If there was anyone that should have been afraid to leave the cabin it was Rebecca, but she locked her emotions back inside and climbed to her feet.

"Take it easy," Josie warned.

Rebecca took a moment to steady herself, still leaning against the bunk. "Hungry..." she said.

Channie rushed back to her own bunk and then came back with a granola bar for Rebecca. She accepted it with gratitude and immediately shoved half of it into her face. Lewis turned away as she hurried to change out of her wet and bloodied clothing. Channie began filling a backpack with more granola bars and bottled water for the hike.

Josie took the moment to talk to Lewis. "You said you were sent to protect me?" she asked. "By who?"

Lewis grimaced. "That's complicated," he said. "What's important right now is that we get you back to Edmonds safely."

Josie had just recently moved to Edmonds, which was about a three hour car ride from the camp. The fact that Lewis apparently knew that about her only added to Josie's wariness of him.

"Those ghasts aren't the brightest, but they aren't the only things out there looking for you tonight," Lewis continued. "And make no mistake, they are here for you." His serious tone was matched with a steely-eyed expression.

Josie's mind flashed upon the tall figure that had been watching the cabin that morning.

"Okay, let's go," said Rebecca through a partially full mouth once she was done changing. She was still munching on the same bite of granola bar.

Channie joined them at the door. "Will they be alright?" she asked, talking quietly as she gestured to the rest of the girls who were still watching them with worried faces.

Lewis's expression did not exude confidence. "They'll be better off with us gone," he said. Their group turned to look at the other girls, confusion and worry abound. Lewis cleared his throat. "We are going to go get help for Rebecca," he said. "You should all stay inside for your own safely, at least until morning." None of the other girls said anything. They all continued to stare at Lewis as if he were an alien. "Alright then."

Lewis quickly "borrowed" a flashlight from out of a bag near him and was the first through the door, soon followed by Josie, Rebecca, and Channie.

Outside, the wind whipped at their faces, carrying with it an uncomfortable spray of fine raindrops. Lewis put his hood up while the girls wrapped their coats tightly around themselves.

The sky had become overcast, hiding the aurora borealis, but flashes of lightning popped periodically, revealing an orange hue that looked reminiscent of wildfire smoke. The glow of the atmosphere had an eerie apocalyptic look about it.

The wind and rain forced them to keep their faces aimed downward as they trudged across the camp, with the exception of Lewis, in the lead, who kept his eyes on the trees and sky despite his clear discomfort. They had to maintain a slow pace for Rebecca. Every step was a challenge for the poor girl, but she did not complain even once. They all had seen what was out there, and they all knew the stakes if they did not get as far away from the camp as possible.

By the time they reached the edge of camp, they still had not come across anyone else. The bobcat lockdown was in full effect and the hour was getting late. They continued on down the aptly named Camp Orkila Road until they came to a split.

"I don't actually know the way to the ferry," Lewis admitted.

Channie took over the lead. "It's that way," she said, "the same way they bussed us in from."

"I didn't arrive by bus," said Lewis.

Channie looked at him weird, but didn't inquire further. They continued on down Darvill Farm Road to the east, entering a clear-cut area with no trees (or cover) on either side of the road. It was easier to see that nothing was hiding off to the sides, but they were also fully exposed. After a little over a quarter mile straightaway, the road made an abrupt turn due south.

Lewis paused briefly, staring out behind them. "I think something is following us," he said.

Josie scanned the road and sky behind them but couldn't see anything. A knot of fear clenched her insides.

"Don't shine your lights back," said Lewis. "It ducked down in the ditch." He searched the road ahead for somewhere for them to hide. "Quick, this way," he said.

They hurried south to where a farmhouse stood near the road and ducked against the side of the structure. Everyone turned off their flashlights and waited on bated breath to see what would come around the bend in the road. The wind was still howling, covering up any sounds that may have been made by whatever was approaching.

With eyes wide and straining they watched along the bend for any sign of motion. The rain continued to beat down on them. Josie wiped her face slowly to clear her vision. She didn't want to move too quickly, fearing that it might call attention to their group.

After several minutes passed in silence, a singular dark form shifted slowly into Josie's line of sight. With nothing but dirt on either side of the road, it was difficult to tell how large the figure was, but Josie could tell it was walking upright on two legs. It paused upon noticing the absence of Josie's group from their expected trajectory.   The shadow remained absolutely still for what felt like forever, daring them to make the first move.

Without warning it started running with shuffling footsteps that could be heard over the wind. The footfalls slapped against the pavement as the figure continued on down the road. It wasn't until it was directly in front of the farmhouse that Josie recognized Steph's blonde ponytail bouncing back and forth and was able to breathe a sigh of relief.

Rebecca groaned upon realizing who it was. Steph still hadn't noticed them.

"That little…" mumbled Channie, "I'm gunna—" she didn't finish her sentence before jumping up from their hiding place. "Roar!"

Steph fell sideways, landing on her butt in the middle of the street. She burst into tears a second later when she realized it was just Channie.

"What are you doing out here?" asked Josie.

Channie helped Steph back up to her feet. Steph wiped her tears with the back of her hand as several flashlights lit her face. She sniffled grossly as she scowled at everyone. "They killed Jerry," she said

Channie grimaced, instantly feeling bad about scaring her.

Steph scrunched her eyebrows up angrily. "I overheard you guys talking about needing to get out of here, so I followed you. You have to tell me, what's really out there? What killed Jerry?"

All eyes turned towards Lewis. There was no getting around explaining what he knew this time. He took a deep breath before speaking. "They're actually what the myth of vampires came from," he said without batting an eye. "Night Terrors, ghasts, vampires. They are flying predators with deadly claws and a thirst for blood. They see poorly but have acute hearing and hunt at night. And… apparently can sound like crying children to lure in their victims."

"How do you know all this?" asked Steph.

"I read it in a very convincing book," said Lewis. "We should keep moving. We're not safe yet."

Lewis has been taking notes from me! He tells the girls just enough to keep moving forward without drowning in the details. There weren't so many night terrors around these woods on other attempts at this journey.... The Agares are narrowing in on our would-be heroes. They are sending through into the mortal realm a horde of nightmarish proportion. I'm not sure I will be able to withhold my manipulation for much longer with all the new pieces coming into play.... If they manage to Erase these kids from existence, it truly is a grim future for all of humanity. I wish I could have done more to prepare each of them for what is to come, but the tides of war wait for no man.

Keep vigilant,

-Mr. Gray

CHAPTER

10

A Safe Place

With Steph added to the group, they trudged on through the darkness, quickly passing beyond the farm property and back into densely packed forest on either side of the road. The trees provided some much needed cover from the unpleasant wind.

Lewis was the only one in the group not wearing a proper coat. His plain cloth hoodie was already soaked through and heavy with rain. The cold was weighing on him, though he did his best not to show it.

Josie mused briefly at how easily the older white boy had gotten four young girls to follow him away from camp in the dark of night. It was a terrible and not well-enough known statistic that indigenous women go missing and are killed at a much higher rate per capita than any other societal group. Josie wasn't looking to become one of the numbers.

She sincerely doubted that Lewis had the capacity to human-traffic her, though, nor the wherewithal; he hadn't even managed to dress himself properly for the weather. No, Lewis was not her worry.

The vampiric ghasts on the—other hand, along with whatever else was out there, could very easily end her life without raising any rippling societal concerns, apparently. Knowing that fact didn't make Josie feel any less crummy about her current predicament. At best, having Steph with them with her blonde hair and blue eyes might just give them a shot at something beyond a quick forty second segment on the regional nightly news if they ended up going missing.

If they didn't make it out, either the storm or the make-believe bobcat would be blamed for their disappearance. It would make a tragic and wholly forgettable story.

Josie glanced over at Rebecca. She was looking a little worse for wear. Her posture was slumped horribly and she was walking with an obvious limp. When Josie moved closer to her, she could hear Rebecca muttering to herself in an unintelligible murmur under her breath. She spoke quickly in what Josie could only assume was a mantra of some sort.

Her murmurs grew suddenly into a fully voiced word: "Thirsty," she rasped. She immediately stumbled to her side and would have fallen over had Josie not been there to help steady her feet.

Channie came to her aid, retrieving one of the bottles of water from her backpack. Rebecca snatched the bottle from Channie with unexpected ferocity, discarding the cap to the ground as she twisted it open. She chugged the entire bottle down in one go.

Rebecca dropped the empty bottle and continued on forward, shuffling her feet as if in a daze. Josie and Channie looked at each other, silently sharing their concern. A distant scream rang out behind them, carried their direction by the wind. They remained on edge. There was nothing to do but to keep moving forward.

They hiked on for several more miles down the wooded road until Rebecca stumbled even worse, this time falling completely to the ground. She groaned as everyone came over to her side to help pick her back up. She wasn't able to continue walking without assistance after that. Eventually Rebecca stopped moving her feet altogether and the other girls had to start taking turns helping Lewis drag her along down the road.

"We can't keep this up for long," complained Steph as she quickly became exhausted. "We need to find a safe place."

She wasn't wrong. They wouldn't be able to make it all the way to the ferry dock without taking a break. They kept going, though, until another section of farm land opened up before them. They all headed for the nearest structure without the need for discussion. It was difficult to see in the darkness. It wasn't until they reached the empty barn that they realized that it was in fact a barn rather than a farmhouse that they had landed upon.

Several more horrifying cries at their backs added fuel to their haste. The ghasts' screams came from different directions, rising over the din of the storm. They were searching. Hunting. Lewis boosted Channie up to an unlatched window. She crawled in and was around the corner opening the door for everyone else a few moments later. The metal door squealed at its hinges as it swung open. Everyone piled inside and shut the door behind them.

The barn had a loft and stacks of hay in several piles. Various rakes and other tools hung on one wall between nail pegs. The window Channie climbed in through was the only window in the whole structure, and it faced south, away from the direction of camp and the ghasts.

They plopped Rebecca down on one of the hay piles. The girls stripped off their wet coats while Lewis went over to the window. He attempted to close it, but found that its housing was warped and the pane could only close to the same gap with which they had discovered it.

Channie and Josie approached Lewis to discuss their plan.

"We'll need to get moving again before dawn in order to make it to the ferry in time," said Channie.

Lewis nodded. "I guess this is as good of a place as any to hunker down for a couple hours," he said.

Steph was hunched over Rebecca, inspecting her with her flashlight. Concern flecked Steph's eyes as she took in the dark veins spiderwebbing across Rebecca's face and neck. Her expression changed to disgust as a froth of spit bubbles dribbled out from Rebecca's mouth. "I don't think she's alright..." said Steph.

Everyone grouped around Rebecca. Her eyes were squeezed shut tight. Her breaths came steady, but quick. Her face was very pale, still damp with rain and her hair was slicked to her forehead. No one knew what to do for her.

"Whatever's happening, hopefully rest will help…" said Lewis.

Everyone spread out, trying to find comfy spots amongst the hay. Josie approached Lewis, seeking more answers from the mysterious boy. He was laid back on a pile with his arms behind his head, but he did not look relaxed. His face held a wary expression, but lit up as Josie came over. She sat down next to him and leaned onto her side, folding her legs together.

"Are you going to tell me what's going on now?" Josie asked.

Lewis's eyes drifted towards Josie's lips. They lingered there for a long moment. "Most people wouldn't believe the truth," he said as he remade eye contact with her. "But you aren't like most people." His gaze seemed to stare into her soul.

Josie's heart fluttered.

"I've come back from about a year in the future," he said with a straight face.

Josie narrowed her eyes.

"It's true!" Lewis insisted. "We know and trust each other by then. You tell me about Adeona."

Josie's breath caught in her chest. She hadn't spoken that name out loud since early on in therapy after her parents' deaths. Her chest felt tight, her stomach flipping at the memory. It no longer surprised her that she'd woken from that particular nightmare that very morning. It was intuition, preemptively preparing her for the triggering day that was to unfold.

She'd always mostly known that Adeona was real—that her experiences with the creature hadn't just been inside her head—but she'd never had such solid confirmation before. Silent tears streamed down her face unabated.

"I'm sorry," said Lewis. "I know the memories are painful."

She wasn't crying because it was painful. She was simply overwhelmed. She continued to stare into Lewis's eyes, searching his face for any sign of misgiving.

Lewis reached over with his fingertips and gently brushed the tears from Josie's cheeks. They continued to gaze at one another until Lewis leaned in and planted a small, off-center peck on Josie's lips. He withdrew slightly, gauging her response. Josie leaned forward, and kissed Lewis back, longer this time.

A rush of energy tingled through Josie's body. It felt as if a weight had been lifted off her chest. She could finally breathe again. The heat of Lewis's own breath filled Josie's lungs as their lips met together in a desperate dance. Josie's tears began flowing again at the familiarity Lewis exuded across every tender movement.

She couldn't explain the feeling inside of her, bubbling up like carbonation in her lungs. She soaked up every exhilarating moment of it, her heart racing again, this time with desire.

Lewis wiped her tears away again. Josie latched onto him when he was done, laying the side of her head down on his shoulder. He squeezed back onto her just as snugly.

It was a comforting position despite his soggy hoodie. Josie finally allowed herself to rest for the first time that day. Despite all the danger that surrounded them, she somehow felt safe in Lewis's arms. Their breathing slowed as they laid together, sharing warmth. Eventually Josie fell asleep lying against Lewis's chest.

I looked away during the mushy stuff. Those two really can't control themselves around each other, can they? It's the potential of their spark which caught my eye so very long ago. You do know, I've been at this for way longer than most Parcae have the patience to hang around. It's a tough job being a Fate. You all are very lucky I enjoy your realm so much. Without the unfettered love these kids have for each other to push them on through the hard times, the Agares would have managed to snip your realm from existence long ago. I hope it will be enough this time for their final attempt at salvation.

Keep vigilant,

-Mr. Gray

CHAPTER

11

A Hero or a Maniac

Josie awoke to Lewis vigorously shaking her. It was still dark. Her face was damp where it had been resting against Lewis's chest, and not just from the rain. A slick puddle of drool strung between them as they separated.

Josie wiped her face with the back of her hand, severing the slobber trail as she turned away in embarrassment. She hardly had time to ground herself in the moment when Lewis leapt up to his feet and gestured for her to follow. He crept silently over to where the other girls were resting. Josie followed him over in the dark, scanning her eyes across the dense shadows of the barn as they consolidated the group. Channie and Steph sat up as they approached. Rebecca didn't rise. She appeared to be sleeping, fatigue having gotten the better of her.

"Did you guys hear that?" whispered Lewis, barely audible as he pointed up towards the loft.

Channie and Steph shook their heads.

Josie turned her attention upwards. The loft exuded only stillness. She'd heard nothing since waking up. Everybody huddled together now, staring towards the shadowed area above. A gust of wind outside produced a whistling draft somewhere unseen. The wind was getting in up there. And if the wind could get in…

Heh-heh-heh!

—A shrill chuckle sounded from out of the darkness above.

Woo-woah!

—A breathy sob of a response cried out from the opposite side of the loft. There was already more than one inside!

Josie was grateful no one had made any noise or turned on their flashlights. The creatures were talking to each other in the dark, seemingly unaware of the frightened children below.

Thump-thump thump-thump thump-thump!

—A series of quick footfalls pounded against the floor of the overhanging loft. The scampering ceased directly above the children. The silence that followed didn't help ease their terror.

Josie held her breath, not daring to make a sound. Steph, seated beside her, appeared to be on the verge of a panic attack. Her eyes were wide with fear. The beginnings of hyperventilation showed in the girl's rhythms with tiny puffs of air blasting through her flared nostrils.

A heavy thud against the stuck-open window on the other side of the barn produced a scream from Steph. Channie muffled Steph's cry with the palm of her hand, but the damage was already done.

A chorus of excited cries rang out from above. It sounded like a pair of unruly kindergartners cackling. The old barn creaked and groaned as the ghasts clamored over to the railing, chittering joyfully all the while. In the same moment another thud at the window was punctuated by the crash of glass shattering.

Lewis flicked on his flashlight. The beam cut through the darkness, revealing two ghasts climbing upside down over the loft's railing. They clung to the overhang with their feet like giant bats. A third creature was inside by the broken window. It picked itself up and scampered across the barn floor sending bits of broken glass skittering about. The two ghasts dangling from the overhang froze in place as Lewis's light landed upon them, blinding their nocturnally inclined eyes. Their jagged-toothed maws stretched wide as they hissed towards the unexpected light source.

Lewis raised his arm with the silver coil wrapped around it. He pointed his wrist towards the dangling ghasts. As soon as he flexed his arm, a flash of energy like a bolt of lightning shot out from his wrist, barely missing one of the ghasts.

The creatures retreated in a flurry of wing-flaps and flailing limbs. They whooped like hyenas as they pulled themselves back up and over the railing.

Lewis turned towards the third ghast, letting more energy blasts fly. The barn lit up with the flashes. The blasts sounded in low resonating booms as the light dissipated against the far wall of the barn.

The two monsters up above swooped down simultaneously with wings spread wide. Steph and Channie scattered, screaming as they went in opposite directions. Lewis pushed Josie behind him. She fell down in the hay beside Rebecca, who was still unconscious.

Lewis dropped his flashlight to the barn floor. He used his newly freed hand to pull a tiny whistle out from under his shirt and placed it between his lips. No sound was produced as he blew hard through the opening, but all three ghasts reacted violently, shaking immediately with intense spasms.

The two that were swooping down crashed to the floor hard, while the third fell over writhing and hissing. Whatever sound the whistle was making, only the monsters were able to hear it.

Unfortunately, the distraction only lasted a moment before the ghasts picked themselves back up and moved again towards the children, even more angrily.

Josie scooped up Lewis's flashlight, aiming it at the ghasts to give Lewis some light to guide his energy blasts.

Across the barn, the third ghast narrowed in on Steph over by the side wall. She groped wildly through the darkness at the tools hanging between nails. A wooden handle fell into her grasp. She swung towards the ghast as it lunged at her. The bristles of a broom-head slapped the ghast across its snout, narrowly diverting its chomp.

It turned back towards Steph slowly, chuckling all the while.

Steph struck it again.

The broom-head broke off with the powerful swing. The creature stopped laughing. Its black scales bristled, glistening in the flashes of light as Lewis fired upon the other two monsters. It reared up on its hind legs and snatched the broom handle from Steph with its fast fingers. It brought the stick down with a sharp crack against its own knee, snapping it in half effortlessly.

The ghast lunged at Steph's neck with snapping teeth. A shout from Channie distracted its attack while a pitchfork to its back ended its life. Channie grunted as she stabbed the creature through.

Across the barn, Lewis was having difficulty hitting his targets. They dodged his attacks, dashing left and right. Lewis shifted to the side, trying to draw the monsters away from Josie and Rebecca.

"Over here! Come get me!" Lewis yelled. He blew into his whistle again.

It was working! The ghasts screamed back at Lewis with terrifying high-pitched screeches that pierced the night.

A groan from Rebecca stole Josie's attention. Rebecca was sitting up, pale as a corpse. She was attempting to climb to her feet. Josie moved in and helped steady her.

"I need light!" cried Lewis as he stumbled backwards, away from the attacking monsters.

Josie found him again with the flashlight. The ghasts dodged between support posts, quickly closing in on Lewis.

A well-timed blast of energy collided with one of the monsters. A brilliant glow flashed out from the creature like an exploding star. By the time Josie's eyes readjusted to the darkness, the ghast ceased to exist. Erased. Plucked from the multi-verse, including from the memories of each of the girls. Only Lewis, outside of his native time steam, remembered that the creature had ever been.

Josie watched as the *one* ghast from the loft deftly out-maneuvered Lewis's wildly inaccurate energy blasts.

Lewis zeroed in on his target as Josie steadied her flashlight across the creature's advance. It dove at him, screeching. Lewis lit it up with a blast from his coil. The ghast flashed brilliantly, briefly blinding Josie and confusing her.

Lewis's odd behavior—acting like a maniac, shooting flashes of light into the darkness while Channie and Steph dealt with the *lone* ghast all by themselves—was wholly unhelpful.

Josie scowled at him from across the barn as she shifted her weight to better aid Rebecca's slumping stance. Rebecca hissed quietly as she rounded on Josie and sank her full mouth of teeth into the exposed flesh of Josie's neck.

The terrible pinch was shocking, like ice water in her veins. She went weak in the knees as Rebecca tore into her viciously. Josie gasped. She could feel her blood spilling down her body; her warmth leaving her.

Josie crumpled into the hay pile. Everything went dark as she fell on the flashlight. Her mind went fuzzy as she drifted into delirium. She was on the verge of passing out. Her breath quickened in her chest as the world slipped away like the tide through outstretched fingers.

Images came back to her like waves crashing upon her. A tiny man—a Parca, standing beside her; Lewis pulling Rebecca away from her; the girls huddling around her as the Fate injected a metallic fluid that looked like mercury into her arm.

The liquid silver serum burned like acid in her veins.

The world slipped away into darkness again.

Okay, okay, I couldn't just stand by and let Josie succumb to the madness. Things are playing out more dangerously than ever before.... Previous attempts at this journey didn't require my direct attention until the following day. I apologize for not explaining this before, but Lewis has in his possession several other-worldly devices: A whistle whose pitch creatures from beyond the mortal realm can't stand but which humans cannot hear, and a silver coil wrapped around his wrist that is capable of Erasing anything its energy blasts touch. Once Erased, only people outside of their native time stream (in this case only Lewis and myself) have any memory that they ever existed in the first place. Now please excuse me, for I have several pressing matters to attend to! Hang in there Josie!

Keep vigilant,

-Mr. Gray

CHAPTER

12

Tucked Away

Josie sensed stillness around her as she awoke in darkness. She felt enclosed, as if in a tomb. Her neck twinged where Rebecca bit her, sending a spike of pain down her arm. It was unpleasant, but minor compared to the excruciating lava that had filled her body before she passed out.

She had no frame of reference, but it felt like it had been a long time since the attack. Her eyes were practically glued shut with crust. She rubbed them as she sat up, nearly bumping her head on a low rock ceiling.

"Welcome back," said a tiny, high-pitched voice in the darkness.

Her eyes could just barely perceive the outline of the doll-sized Fate standing before her. Being in the presence of a Parca again after so many years of therapy filled Josie's heart with dread. She began breathing quickly as a torrent of emotions crashed down upon her. Her parents were dead because of Parcae meddling. It was all too real.

"Where am I?" Josie demanded as she scooted away from the creature. She didn't stop until her back touched the cave wall.

"Tucked away," said the Parca. His eyes shined red in the darkness. "This is a time pocket," he said plainly, as if that explained anything.

Josie stared back at the unblinking creature.

"My name is Mr. Gray. Not that you asked," he said. "We are about to have a long history together—"

"—How do I get out of here?" Josie interrupted.

Mr. Gray took a step closer. Josie flinched. "Calm down," said Mr. Gray. "Time pockets are like eddies in the river of time. You needed time. And it moves in circles here. So now you've had time to recover from your near-case of Vampirism." Mr. Gray let out a chuckle. "Lewis, under my guidance, stuffed you in this hole to save your life."

"How. Do. I. Get. Out?!" Josie felt pressure building inside of her; a claustrophobic twinge.

Mr. Gray sighed. "Now that you've awoken I can go tell Lewis to retrieve you." The Parca began to recede into the darkness, but then paused. "You needn't fear my kind—most of us, anyway. A war rages outside of your time stream, and the Parcae have not given up on the mortal realm just yet, despite the high cost."

Josie didn't know what to say.

"I'll see you again soon," Mr. Gray said ominously. His tiny shoes echoed against the stone of the cave floor as he fully disappeared into the darkness. "Oh, and don't try to leave until you are retrieved," he added. "Otherwise you won't come out at the right time…."

Josie didn't like the sound of that. "Retrieved? How?" But Mr. Gray was already gone.

Impenetrable silence fell across her. The stone crevice that surrounded Josie was cold and stagnant. It was an empty place. A dead place. A void outside of time itself.

There was nothing to do but wait. Josie focused on steadying her breath. She settled down to the cave floor and tried to pretend she was somewhere else—anywhere else. She squeezed her eyes shut and placed an ear to the ground.

The stone came alive beneath her. A low rumble grew like the dull vibration of a clamoring train in the distance. The rumble deepened until she could feel it clearly in her clenched jaw.

A bright light suddenly filled Josie's vision, sliding steadily nearer. It took a moment for her eyes to adjust, and then another moment for her to understand what she was looking at. A wooden pallet on wheels lurched to a stop beside her. A flashlight was strapped to it and a trailing rope attached it to the outside world.

Josie sat down squarely on the pallet and gave the rope a quick tug to signal she was there. The rope drew taught and began to pull Josie up the slight incline of the bumpy cave floor. The flashlight shined across Rebecca, unconscious, lying against the opposite wall of the chamber. The pallet did not pause in its course. It was not yet Rebecca's time to leave this place.

A shift in the air brought a condensing chill. It felt like stepping off a plane in Seattle; a sudden change in pressure and humidity. The sounds of the outside world fell upon Josie once more as if she'd just emerged from underwater.

Lewis, Channie, and Steph came into view, all lined up, hands working hard to pull in the rope. Sunlight streamed past foliage behind them and down into the crevasse. Mr. Gray was perched on a tree branch above. Lewis glanced over at the pale-skinned, flat-faced creature. Mr. Gray's button-down patchwork jacket and brown trousers wrinkled as he crouched upon the branch in silence. Neither Channie nor Steph seemed to be aware of his presence judging by their unperturbed faces.

The Parcae were invisible to humans. It was only after choosing to reveal oneself that the species could be perceived at all. That was how Adeona had explained it to Josie anyway. Adeona's presence in her childhood meant that the Parcae could no longer hide from her.

Everyone stopped pulling on the rope as soon as Josie was clear of the tight opening. Lewis rushed over and helped her climb to her feet.

Still crouched nonchalantly above, Mr. Gray cleared his throat. "Send me back down for Rebecca," he said.

Lewis reached up and retrieved him. He placed Mr. Gray on the wooden pallet.

"She's not conscious yet," said Josie.

"Time flows differently in there," said Mr. Gray. "She'll be ready."

Lewis gave him a shove. The pallet bounded back down into the crack like a bobsled.

"You shouldn't trust him," said Josie as soon as Mr. Gray was out of earshot.

Lewis smiled to himself, dismissing Josie's concern. "He's fine. It's the Agares we need to worry about."

"What are you talking about?" asked Channie.

"I really don't understand what's going on," said Steph.

Lewis grimaced. It must have looked strange to the other girls—as if Lewis had mimed his interaction with the Parca.

Josie shook her head. "He's dangerous…." Her voice faltered, the words bubbling up meekly.

Lewis gripped onto Josie's hands and locked eyes with her. "It's okay," he said softly. "I know what you've been through, but he's one of the good guys. I won't let anything bad happen to you."

Josie felt the urge to shy away from Lewis's gaze, but she held strong, searching his face for any sign of insincerity. He released her hands but stayed close to her.

"That's some intense eye contact," said Channie.

Lewis's cheeks turned pink, but a tiny smile cracked his lips. "I'm glad you're okay."

A tug at the rope signaled that Rebecca was in position. Everyone began pulling again. Josie joined in, heaving Rebecca out of the time pocket.

When Rebecca emerged she was sitting cross-legged with Mr. Gray in her lap. She was still looking unusually pale, but beamed a smile up at Josie as she came into view.

The bite mark on Josie's neck twinged.

"Hey," said Rebecca, "I'm really sorry… I don't remember much, but this little demon says I'm a Vampire now."

"I'm going to have to insist that somebody explains what is going on," said Steph.

"Could you just reveal yourself to them already?" Lewis asked Mr. Gray.

Mr. Gray hopped out of Rebecca's lap. "Fine," he said. "But then it's time to hustle to the ferry." Mr. Gray spun in a quick circle before posing with wiggling fingers. "Ta-dah!"

Steph screamed as Mr. Gray appeared in front of her.

Channie stared wide-eyed at the tiny creature.

"He's a friend," said Lewis.

Channie blinked several times in dismay.

Steph quieted down and moved in for a closer look despite her shock. "A tiny man!"

"He's a Fate," said Lewis. "He knows the future, and will be helping us survive."

"I know I'm a novelty," said Mr. Gray, "but if you all don't make haste to the ferry, your futures will be disappointingly short." He marched off into the woods without another wasted moment.

Rebecca, looking particularly spry, jumped up and hurried after the little creature. Lewis and Josie were not far behind, leaving Channie and Steph exchanging bewildered expressions.

I didn't want to frighten the children too much, but they tend to chatter less on the next leg of the journey when they are a bit scared. Less small talk isn't really an advantage to the outcome, but it is a reprieve to my ears. One can only listen to teenage girls squabbling over the same social drama so many times before silence really does become the greatest virtue. That's not to say the net isn't closing in on the children though. The danger is real. New occurrences are rare when you've been through it all before like I have. A new occurrence usually provides opportunity to a Parca, but the Agares horde pouring into the mortal realm is not a welcome addition to this day. So much is changing faster than I can keep track of it! I wasn't even supposed to be here for this part of the journey!

Keep vigilant,

-Mr. Gray

CHAPTER

13

Vampires 101

As the children trudged out of the woods Rebecca eyed the bright sky tentatively. "As a *Vampire*, should I be concerned…?" She gestured toward the sun.

Mr. Gray, being carried by Lewis now, chuckled boisterously. "You'll be fine," he said, "but sunscreen is always a good idea."

Everyone had taken meeting the Parca in stride, though Steph was staring at him now as if he would disappear if she took her eyes off him.

It took half the remaining walk to the ferry for Josie to realize it wasn't only Mr. Gray that had Steph so captivated. She was staring at Lewis just as much.

"What's that thing around your wrist?" Steph finally asked.

Lewis shifted his sleeve to hide the silver coil from sight. "It's a weapon," he said.

Steph nodded absently. "It looked like fireworks were shooting out of your hand last night."

Lewis readjusted Mr. Gray in his arms. "Anything I shoot with it ceases to have ever existed."

"Oh," said Steph. "Okay."

Josie wondered what Lewis had been shooting at. To her, he had appeared to be firing wildly at nothing, but if she was to believe what he was saying, he had been shooting at things that no longer existed…. It was all very strange to think about.

"We don't want to know what's out there, do we?" asked Channie.

Rebecca shuddered. She had a better idea than the rest of them. The night terrors had fed on her.

Josie could no longer see any evidence of the wounds on Rebecca's skin. Her stint in the time pocket had been transformative.

"What about wooden stakes to the heart or garlic?" asked Rebecca. "Or crucifixes, or silver bullets?"

Mr. Gray nodded absently. "Wooden stakes would have killed you before the Vampirism, so no change there. Silver bullets is a werewolf thing, and werewolves don't really exist, so that's irrelevant. Garlic might actually taste even better now to you though, so that one's a plus. You'll also be slightly faster and stronger than before and have a good immune system." He waved his hand dismissively through the air. "Holy symbols are also inert. Being a vampire isn't like it is in the movies."

"Anything else I should know for the future?" asked Rebecca.

Mr. Gray looked contemplative for a moment. "Avoid fake banana flavoring," he said with a slow nod of his head.

"You're mildly allergic. You usually don't figure that one out until you're thirty."

"Hmm," said Rebecca.

"Yeah. Hives," said Mr. Gray.

"Am I gunna be rich??" asked Steph.

Channie laughed. "The priorities on this girl!"

Mr. Gray turned his head slowly to meet Steph's gaze. "Perhaps—if you live through the day."

Steph's eyes grew wide.

"I'll do my best to help," said Mr. Gray.

They continued on in perturbed silence as a line of cars waiting for the first ferry of the day came into view ahead. The ferry was already docked, but was still unloading cars.

"Anyone have money for the fare?" asked Lewis once they reached the terminal building.

"No need," said Mr. Gray. "A red pickup truck will be joining the back of the line shortly. There's a tarp to hide under. Just wait for the driver to use the restroom."

No sooner had he spoken than the red truck appeared around a bend in the road. Their timing couldn't have been any better. The pickup joined the short line of cars outside the ferry terminal. The driver was an older gentleman with white hair. He got out and headed into the terminal building, giving the group of children plenty of time to climb into the truck bed unnoticed.

Everyone squeezed together, shimmying beneath a blue tarp before the old man returned. Josie found herself pressed up against Lewis with Mr. Gray cradled between them like a baby.

Lewis had a lost puppy-dog look on his face. He rested his hand tenderly on her hip, holding onto her.

"You guys are cute," said Mr. Gray.

The corners of Lewis's mouth pulled back slightly into an embarrassed grimace. His cheeks reddened as Josie subconsciously bit at her lip.

Josie felt the energy—a nervous buzz like the tingle of caffeine in her stomach. Lewis's obvious admiration for Josie was matched by her budding curiosity in him.

He claimed to know her in the future. It sounded so absurd, and yet, she believed him. She felt safe with him, despite the omnipresent threat of inter-dimensional monsters. Even Mr. Gray's creepy little face staring up at her couldn't spoil the moment.

After loading onto the ferry, Channie texted her mom to ask her to come pick them up across the water in Anacortes. Mrs. Davis responded with confusion and concern, but ultimately a ride was on the way. They stayed in place at Mr. Gray's behest, waiting until the driver of the car behind them stepped out to stretch his legs before making any moves. It was almost time for the ferry to unload. One by one they began to sneak out of the truck to join the walk-on passengers.

Everything was going perfectly to plan. Rebecca went first, nonchalantly slipping out from under the tarp and stepping gently over the passenger side of the vehicle without alerting the driver. Channie went next, slinking away just as smoothly. When it came to Steph's turn, however, her foot caught on the edge of the truck bed and she banged against the side with a noticeable thud.

Steph ducked down as the old man glanced in his rearview mirror.

Mr. Gray's expression shifted, flashing a hint of concern. "Wait here until I signal for you," he said. He climbed over Lewis's legs and hopped into Steph's awaiting arms. The odd pair moved in tandem, Mr. Gray directing Steph on the optimal path between vehicles to avoid notice.

Lewis shimmied over and peeked out from under the tarp. By the time Steph and Mr. Gray were clear, he could already see the driver of the car behind them coming back. Mr. Gray in the distance shook his head wildly back and forth at Lewis. It was already too late. Josie and Lewis were stuck now. There was no way out that wouldn't result in somebody realizing they'd snuck aboard the ferry.

Before they could figure out what to do, the ferry was docked, engines were starting back up again, and the truck was rolling along off the ferry and then down the road too fast for them to do anything but hold on.

Well, well.   This day just keeps getting further and further off-track. I feel like a jazz musician and a circus juggler rolled into one.   I had to toss these kids to the wind, but you best believe everything is still playing to the beat of my song.   I don't want to spoil anything, but the Agares are never far when the fate of our Chosen children is churning. While the Agares are not the most subtle of foes—very heavy handed in their ways if you ask me—they always seem to turn up when and where they are least wanted. Always with the destroying and Erasing. You'll see what I mean soon. They are some of the biggest jerks of the multi-verse. One would think they might have learned some compassion during their development as a species—they are quite ancient—but their thirst for energy has made them terribly adversarial to anyone and everything that stands in their way. They'd repurpose all the energy of the entire multi-verse if left unchecked.

Keep vigilant,

-Mr. Gray

CHAPTER

14

Tentacles

The sputtering rumble of the old truck's diesel engine grew louder as it accelerated down the road. They were going too fast to bail. Lewis peeked out from under the tarp, trying to get a bearing on their direction.

Josie's cellphone buzzed in her pocket. She pulled it out, surprised to see that it still had any battery left. "Hey, it's Steph," read the text from an unknown number. It came in a group chat with Rebecca and Channie included as well. "We r getting into Channie's mom's car. Will b in pursuit. Hang tight!"

Josie read the text to Lewis. He didn't look relieved.

The truck slowed, turning off of the main road. Lewis peered out again, trying to get an eye on the street sign, but it passed by too quickly.

"Tell them we turned off the road," he said with a frown.

Josie passed the vague information along, but no sooner had she pressed send than her phone's screen turned black. The battery was dead.

After about another mile the truck came to a sudden stop, slamming both children against the back of the cabin with a thud. The driver opened his door, hopped out, and yanked the tarp off of them before they could do anything.

The old man looked down on them with stern eyes.

"Uh, sorry," said Lewis, sitting up. There wasn't really any good explanation they could give.

The old man didn't skip a beat. "Where are you going?" he asked. "I can give you a ride."

"Um, sure," said Lewis awkwardly. "Just back to the main road would be great, I guess…."

The man nodded. "I can give you a ride." He hopped spryly back into the driver's seat and started going again with Lewis and Josie still in the back.

Josie looked at Lewis with wide eyes. She'd been about to hop out, expecting to get into the cabin, but nearly fell as the truck lurched forward.

The truck continued on, moving farther away from the main road. There wasn't anywhere convenient to turn around at first, but then they passed a turn-off.

Lewis slid open the tiny back window to the cabin. "Sorry again," he said, "but I meant the road we were on before, back the other way."

The old man nodded. "I can give you a ride."

They passed a second turn-off without pause. The old man put his foot to the floor, accelerating well beyond the speed limit.

Josie gripped onto the side of the truck in fear as her hair whipped around her face in the wind.

"Slow down!" Lewis shouted up to the old man.

They were both relieved momentarily as the truck slowed and pulled off the road, but their concern multiplied when the old man kept driving through the empty field ahead. The tires kicked up a cloud of dust behind them.

"Dude!" yelled Lewis. "We're sorry we snuck onto your truck, just let us off!"

The old man peered back, this time with nervous eyes. "I can give you a ride," he said, repeating the same phrase again with the exact same intonation as before, like some sort of human parrot.

The old man's skin rippled slightly. Unnaturally. *Not human.*

The truck stopped with a skidding lurch just shy of a line of trees.

Josie jumped up the moment they stopped. She pulled camp counselor Matt's belt knife out from her pants. Before she knew what was happening, a long tentacle sprang out from the old man's back and slapped the knife out of her grasp. The tentacle then wrapped around her neck, attempting to choke her. Josie flailed, screaming in terror as she grappled with the slimy appendage. She sunk her teeth into it as it went across her face. Warm blue blood gushed into her mouth as she chomped down hard. The creature hissed in pain as it released her.

Her body shook with adrenaline. The metallic taste of the odd blood nearly made her gag.

Lewis raised his arm, aiming his silver coil at the monster in human flesh. The tentacle whipped back around at him, bashing into Lewis as he fired a burst of energy. The shot missed the monster, instead blowing out both the back and driver's side windows. Several more tentacles sprang at him through the broken window. They flailed violently, knocking Lewis down to the truck bed.

The monster withdrew its tentacles after Lewis fell. It no longer resembled an old man as it collapsed inward on itself, as if melting. The creature deflated into an aquatic-looking octopus-like physique, rippling wildly with a dozen tentacles. Its skin shifted about, changing like a kaleidoscope with a thousand different colors.

Before Lewis could get another shot off from his coil, the creature flopped out of the shattered driver's side window and rolled under the truck.

Josie screamed as she pointed to the treeline. A pair of extremely tall and gangly creatures had emerged from the woods.

"Agares!" cried Lewis.

Josie just caught a glimpse of a humongous reptile stepping out of the forest beside the two slender figures. It looked like an oversized Komodo dragon.

With a disorienting shift, everything suddenly changed around her.

Lewis was now in the driver's seat, his whistle in his mouth. He started the truck while sending blast after blast of energy from his coil through a hole in the suddenly broken windshield.

Around the truck everything shifted again—several times in fact—as if Josie were only witnessing one second out of every ten at best. The snippets of time flashed before her eyes as a fight ensued around the vehicle. It was jarringly confusing. The position of the sun changed—they were headed back the other way now. Dark blood was splattered all over the smashed windshield.

Josie smeared a glob of wetness across her cheek. It appeared during the last shift in reality. The sticky red substance now on her hand was definitely blood. It smelled heavily of iron as she rubbed it between her fingers in a confused daze.

"What is happening?" she yelled up to Lewis as she crawled into the cabin through the back window. The plume of dust behind the truck hid the scene of the conflict at their backs. Steam rose up from the dented truck hood as Lewis drove back up onto the road and sped away.

"There was a basilisk!" Lewis exclaimed. "It's a giant lizard that can freeze time—but it can't affect me because I'm not in my native time stream. This whistle messes with its abilities."

Josie swept some of the broken glass from her seat and buckled herself in beside Lewis. She was still in shock.

"Those crazy-tall bearded guys were Agares. They always come in pairs."

"I only saw one," said Josie.

Lewis shook his head. "There were two. I Erased one, but now the coil isn't working anymore. I think it's broken or out of power or something. I hit the other one with the truck while he was riding the basilisk."

Josie looked back behind them apprehensively but couldn't see any sign of the giant lizard or the tall man.

"I'm not sure if they're dead, but they're injured at least," said Lewis.

Based off the amount of blood on the hood of the truck the monsters were definitely not having a very good day.

Josie wiped some of the blue blood from her chin with the neck of her shirt. It looked like she'd been drinking paint. Her jaw ached from the tentacle wrenching itself free from her bite. She spit a glob of blue into the footwell. "I don't like tentacles."

"You never cease to amaze me," said Lewis with a grin.

Josie gagged as she spit again on the floor.

They weren't even halfway back to the main road when the truck's engine began to sputter. A moment later and it cut out entirely. They quickly came rolling to a permanent stop.

Calamari anyone? Us Parcae really love the jiggly-wriggly stuff! A good juicy grub will satisfy an empty belly any day, but I personally still prefer a good burger. When you have the whole timeline of humanity to explore, there is almost no limit to the goodies one can find to consume! But I digress, these are serious times. Lewis managed to burn his coil out in a fit of terror. You shouldn't blame the boy, though, the Agares are terrible... but... he really was just firing that thing like it had unlimited energy. You don't even want to know how energy intensive it is to wipe a person out of existence. The Agares definitely won't be winning any Green Awards anytime soon. It's a dog-eat-dog multi-verse out there. The Agares would burn through half the energy of the cosmos if it meant being able to steal just a little bit more for themselves. They've really taken the whole industrial complex thing to the extreme.

Keep vigilant,

-Mr. Gray

CHAPTER

15

Blood and Bones (or lack thereof)

Lewis slammed his hands down on the steering wheel in frustration. He cranked the key several times trying to get the truck started again, but the ignition merely clicked without turning over. The truck wasn't going anywhere.

"We need to get back to Edmonds tonight, or else…" said Lewis.

"Or else what?" asked Josie.

"Or else Landon is dead…."

Lewis had some more explaining to do. He inhaled deeply and then let out a sigh. "The Agares are going to erase a boy named Landon. He was a bully to me growing up, but in a previous life he was my best friend, I guess… I don't remember being his friend—it was a life lived and now forgotten due to Mr. Gray's time travel meddling—but I know about it because I have notes that previous versions of me left in a time pocket… it's complicated. He ends up our friend in the future anyway, and his life is in danger today, just like yours was… or is… I'm not sure anymore…" Lewis trailed off. He was staring at Josie's mouth. "You look like you ate a smurf."

Josie spit into the footwell again. "What happened to that tentacle guy?"

Lewis shrugged. "I think I ran over him. I honestly have no idea what that thing even was. Some sort of shapeshifter I guess… the Agares have many agents."

In the distance, a silver sedan was driving towards them from up ahead. To their relief, Channie stuck her head out of the passenger side window. She began waving at them frantically as her mom pulled up beside the disabled truck.

Steph and Rebecca hopped out of the back as Josie and Lewis exited the truck. Mrs. Davis's mouth was hanging open as she stepped out as well, inspecting the damage to the vehicle.

"Oh my God. Did you hit a deer?" She rounded on Channie. "Who is this boy?? Is he even old enough to be driving?"

Rebecca ran over and gave Josie a hug. "Are you alright? What happened?"

Josie shook her head. "Do you have any water?" she asked. "I need to rinse my mouth out."

"We have bottles in the trunk," said Channie.

Josie and Lewis followed Channie to the back of the sedan while Mrs. Davis stared in disbelief at all the blood covering the grill of the truck and what was left of the windshield.

Josie quickly cracked open a fresh bottle of water and immediately sloshed half of it onto her face. She swished repeatedly until all the blue blood was gone from her teeth.

Channie knew better than to ask what it was. "Mr. Gray disappeared through a hole in the air," she said in a hushed voice so her mom wouldn't hear.

Lewis nodded absently. "He does that."

Mrs. Davis joined the kids at the back of her car. "Someone's going to have to start explaining some things around here," she said.

Lewis met her glare with a blank expression. "We need to hurry," he said. "My friend is in danger."

Mrs. Davis narrowed her eyes at the boy.

"Please," said Lewis. "We aren't safe here. I'll explain on the road, but we need to go now."

Mrs. Davis put her hands on her hips. "I don't trust you and I don't like you."

"Mama!" cried Channie.

"Fine," said Mrs. Davis, "but you best start talking. Damn crazy kids running off from camp!"

Everyone piled into the car. Channie took shotgun, leaving the rest of the kids to cram into the back. There was only room for three to buckle in, so Josie ended up in Lewis's lap. Rebecca and Steph squished in beside them behind the driver's seat.

Mrs. Davis frowned at Lewis through the rearview mirror as she started the car. Suddenly Steph came running out from behind the truck waving her arms. All eyes shifted towards the back seat where another Steph was already seated.

Without hesitation, Rebecca's fist sprang out and smashed Steph right between the eyes. Her whole hand sunk into

Steph's face, collapsing it like a papier-mâché covered balloon. Her body deflated, morphing into the tentacle covered creature.

The car filled with screams as Rebecca whaled on the shapeshifter repeatedly. Tentacles flailed momentarily and then went limp as the creature was quickly overcome by Rebecca's ferocity.

"I knew I smelled something *off* about her!" Rebecca exclaimed.

"Oh hell nah!" yelled Mrs. Davis as she hopped back out of the car.

The creature was still pulsating with breath, but it was no longer conscious. In its aquatic-looking form, it was only about the size of an Australian Shepard. Its body slumped into a pile of jelly with no bones to hold its shape.

Everyone exited the car again. They stood in silence, staring at the strange creature through the window as its tentacles twitched about, feeling around on the backseat as if they had minds of their own.

Lewis took initiative. He opened the door to the backseat and scooped up the awkward creature in his arms. "Open the trunk," he said.

Mrs. Davis complied, using her key fob to pop the back.

Lewis tossed the creature in unceremoniously and slammed the trunk shut. "Let's go," he said.

Shapeshifters are glorified cuttlefish if you ask me. The Agares wouldn't be using them if they weren't getting a bit desperate to catch these kids. This one couldn't take a punch, but it still managed to take a psychological toll on the children. When you can't trust your eyes, paranoia can start to creep in. Shapeshifters may not be easy to spot, but you can certainly hear the difference—English is not their first language. It's easier to have a conversation with a parrot. The lesson to be learned here, I guess, is always talk to the shy kid, lest they turn out to be a boneless tentacle monster. That's probably not a very universally useful lesson, but for these kids at least, one should certainly always stay alert when dealing with the Agares.

Keep vigilant,

-Mr. Gray

Ride or Die

The silver sedan rolled down the freeway maintaining the exact speed limit. Mrs. Davis clutched the wheel tightly. Everyone kept their eyes focused on the road. No one dared speak, not wanting to acknowledge the presence of a creature from another world unconscious in the trunk. It was as if talking about it would make it more real, and thus more scary.

Steph, despite not having been in the car with everyone else when the shapeshifter transformed back into an invertebrate, was looking more disturbed than anyone else. Seeing her doppelgänger's face collapse had been uniquely unsettling to her, Josie figured. Steph rolled down the back window, leaned out, retched once, vomiting all over the side of the car, then rolled the window back up without a word.

No one acknowledged the incident.

Mrs. Davis glanced back at Lewis through her rearview mirror. She was too afraid to ask the obvious questions, or perhaps no longer really wanted to know the answers. She glanced away again as soon as Lewis returned eye contact with her reflection.

Lewis wasn't inclined to offer up any details about their situation unprompted. The silence was palpable. After several more minutes the tension finally grew to the point where Mrs. Davis could bare it no longer.

"Did you kids summon a demon?" she asked with a straight face. "Is there a demon in the trunk?" She turned towards Channie with an incredulous look on her face. "How many times have I told you not to mess with that ouija tarot voodoo?!"

"No! We didn't summon anything," said Channie. "At least I didn't…."

Mrs. Davis's eyes shifted back towards Lewis in the rearview.

"It's not a demon," he said.

"An alien, then?"

"Not exactly," Lewis sighed. "It doesn't come from space. More like a different plane of existence. A different world in a different timeline."

Lewis might as well have said it was from Hell from the horrified scowl that appeared on Mrs. Davis's face.

Three thuds sounded from the trunk, immediately silencing their chatter.

A raspy voice barely escaped the back. "Where are you going?" It asked. "I… can… give you a ride."

Mrs. Davis gripped the steering wheel tighter.

"A riiiiiiddddeeeeee!" it screeched.

Pounding shook the vehicle as another series of thuds banged like a chorus of thunder.

"That's pretty much all it ever says," said Lewis.

The pounding continued until Channie turned on the stereo to drown it out. An operatic solo poured from the speakers. The creature's squeals quieted down and it stopped banging around as the female vocalist sang loudly in Italian.

After a few minutes Channie tried turning the music down, but the monster in the trunk started banging again almost immediately. This repeated every time she turned it down until she finally gave up and left the opera blasting.

At one point she switched to the radio. Low by Flo Rida filled the car. The creature immediately began banging, but this time it was doing it in time with the music. Channie switched back to the opera cd after the shapeshifter screeched out with the repeat in the music: "With the furrrr!"

As they got closer to Edmonds, Lewis gave Mrs. Davis the address to Josie's house as their destination. Josie was no longer surprised by things like Lewis knowing her address verbatim. When they arrived Josie hopped out and ran inside to retrieve her grandfather.

Mr. Mays came out straight away, taking in all the new faces. Everyone was stretching their legs in the driveway while opera played out muffled from the closed vehicle. He locked eyes with Lewis for a moment before dipping back inside to retrieve a baseball bat from beside the door.

"It's in the trunk," said Josie

Mr. Mays made a beeline for the car. Mrs. Davis joined him at the back. She dangled the keys out to him.

"Watch out, it's wiggly," she said.

Mr. Mays held the bat ready to swing as he popped the trunk.

The old man that was the shapeshifter's original form sat up with a dazed expression on his face. All of the water bottles in the trunk had been emptied and were spread out beneath him. Despite this, his skin looked extremely cracked and dry, appearing halfway mummified in its dehydration.

"Where…give…ride…"

Mrs. Davis slammed the trunk down on the top of its head, knocking it back inside. "Nuh-uh. That's a squid."

Mr. Mays didn't change his expression.

"Water…" the muffled voice begged.

"He's a demon," said Mrs. Davis. There was no doubt behind her eyes. "The boy threw a squid into that trunk."

Mr. Mays nodded absently, contemplating the situation. "Let's take him to the garage…."

A glint of green from the ongoing aurora borealis caught Josie's eye. Things were still not right in the cosmos.

Lewis stepped up behind her and whispered into her ear. "Let's go while they're distracted. We have to get to Landon before it's too late."

Josie wasn't eager to throw herself any deeper into the paranormal activity, but hanging around for a shapeshifter interrogation in her garage hardly seemed less traumatizing.

"I know you don't know Landon yet, but we both need him, and right now, he needs us. He lives just down the road. We can run there."

Josie gave in, following Lewis as he tugged her hand. They slipped away while Mrs. Davis backed the sedan up to the garage.

Oh boy, things are going to start to heat up fast from here. Hold onto your hats and your baseball bats, because the Agares are not going to give up without a fight! I've got to say, I am really impressed with these parents, though. Channie's mom is handling things pretty well for having this all dropped on her in the middle of a hair appointment. One moment you're getting highlights, and then the next you're transporting an other-dimensional creature across county lines. There are no laws against that yet, I checked. A few thousand years in the future, though, things on Earth get a bit more complicated when it comes to the other worldly. Refugees from other dimensions spark new legislation, but it's never very effective. When the Agares snip off a universe, the inhabitants with the means to escape have to go somewhere, ya know?

Keep vigilant,
-Mr. Gray

CHAPTER

17

Instructions Unclear

Josie ran down her street, Lewis leading the way. He held her hand clutched in his, an urgent pace set in his stride. Josie kept up easily—she was a runner with legs built for endurance. She let Lewis pull her along simply because she didn't know where she was going, though she could have just as easily followed behind him. Most substantially, she couldn't help but enjoy the feeling of his hand on hers.

Being around Lewis often made her feel like she'd been picked up by a tornado, but at this point, riding the winds was becoming second nature. At school, Josie was mostly ignored by her peers and she preferred it that way. Middle school was a special kind of hell, especially as a Native American amongst a ninety percent white population. Being a minority already made her stand out, and one should not forget that the phrase *kids can be cruel* was coined specifically in reference to the 'tween years of which Josie was currently plagued.

The matter of the fact was that Josie, riddled with teenage hormones, had not yet been exposed to any form of *positive* male attention by her peers. She was currently known around College Place Middle School as the girl who killed her parents. In hindsight, sharing a version of her story with a girl she thought was her friend had been a mistake. She no longer trusted so easily.

But she trusted Lewis. It was instinctual. Her hand was snug in his. It was so easy to be led along. Lewis had protected her every step of the way so far. She hoped he wouldn't let her down.

Lewis's posture grew tense as he approached a white house on an immaculately landscaped property.

"Stay close," said Lewis.

He stepped up onto the porch and rang the doorbell. After an uncomfortably long moment an older man came to the door. "Hello?" he greeted them.

"Hi, Mr. Mathews, is Landon home?" Lewis asked, anxiety already bubbling up in his voice.

Landon's father blinked several times then lowered his eyebrows into a frown. "I'm sorry, who are you looking for?"

"Landon," said Lewis. "Your son… we're friends."

"I think you have the wrong house," said Mr. Mathews. "I don't have any children."

Lewis's eyes grew wide. "I'm sorry to have bothered you."

Mr. Mathews began to close the door, but hesitated for a moment. "Wait… how do you know my name? You seem familiar…."

"I really must be going," said Lewis. He pulled Josie with him as he backed away from the door.

Mr. Mathews watched them as they hurried back down the driveway and across the road.

"What's going on?" asked Josie.

Lewis's face bore a deep scowl. "We're too late," he said. "The Agares must have Erased Landon already. His own father doesn't remember him...." Lewis began breathing heavily. "This is horrible! How can we be too late!? Without Landon we're all doomed...."

"Ahem..." Mr. Gray cleared his throat. The tiny imp was leaning against a telephone pole just off to their left. "Took you long enough to get here. The Agares came and went nearly an hour ago."

Lewis bounded over to the Parca and scooped him up in his arms. "An hour? An hour ago we were barely off the ferry. There's no humanly possible way I could have made it here in time."

Mr. Gray smiled a big toothy grin. "No worries, all is still going to plan."

"I guess that means I'm going back in time again?" Lewis asked. "But if Landon was Erased, he wouldn't be in any time, no matter how far back I go...."

"That is true," said Mr. Gray. "Once they burn you out of existence, it's retroactive. They are also watching this time period carefully from within the Beyond. No, I cannot take you through time right now, but there is still a way."

"Just tell us," said Josie.

Mr. Gray climbed up Lewis's arm to his shoulder. He stood up tall, gripping onto Lewis's hair for stability. He placed one hand on his hip as he directed a sassy look at Josie. "No patience. You need to learn to take your time when you have time available for the taking. Not all moments contain a big reveal, and the ones that do should be savored when possible."

"What are you getting at?" asked Lewis.

Mr. Gray slid back down into Lewis's arms. "Do you know where your journal is right now?"

Lewis narrowed his eyes. "I left it at the creepy house before you sent me back in time."

Mr. Gray nodded. "And before it was in your possession?"

Lewis shook his head and shrugged slightly. "I got it out of a time pocket."

"And who put it in the time pocket?"

Lewis looked to be putting the puzzle pieces together. "Landon stashed it there for me to find. And a past version of me left it for him to find. Where is this all leading?"

"I'll just jump to the chase," said Mr. Gray. "Landon has the journal stored in the same time pocket you retrieved it from in Yost Park—where an older version of you placed it for him. At this time, it's still there."

Josie blinked in confusion. She didn't understand the point of anything Mr. Gray was saying. "What journal?" she asked.

Mr. Gray and Lewis both turned to look at her.

"You tell her the story," said Mr. Gray, "the abridged version please, I'm growing hungry." His face drooped slightly, already looking bored before Lewis opened his mouth to explain.

"A long time ago, another version of me began to keep a journal of instructions—"

"—Actually…" Mr. Gray interrupted, "technically speaking, all versions of you occupy the same period of time, so this didn't happen a long time ago. You are merely on top of the pile, so-to-speak, at the moment, from your perspective."

"Are you going to tell the story, or are you going to let me do it?" Lewis retorted.

Mr. Gray waved his hand dismissively.

"A long time ago," Lewis repeated, "some version of me that no longer exists wrote down instructions on how to get through his life better and then placed the instructions into a time pocket to be rediscovered back in time by himself. Myself… anyway, by reading the journal, the version of me that did the writing ceased to exist, or really just never came to pass because the version of me reading the journal at a younger age was then able to avoid the mishaps that led to the journal needing to be written in the first place. Are you following this?"

Josie's eyes had gone slightly unfocused as she concentrated. "I think so."

"You looked a little glazed over, there," said Lewis, laughing. "Ok, so what happened was a version of me replaced myself with another version of me which then ran into different problems and amended the instructions and sent them back again, replacing myself over and over again countless times until a journal came into my possession about a year from now for you, which was a few months ago for me." Lewis gestured broadly with one arm.

Mr. Gray was still clutched under his other arm, struggling not to be choked.

Lewis took no notice as he continued on. "I followed the journal to the best of my ability and in doing so have been led here, *on top of the stack.* All the Lewis's that came before tried to escape the Agares but failed in that journey in some way or another. The Agares always won. But now, through pure brute force trial and error over uncountable lifetimes we find ourselves amidst an unlikely Hail Mary of a final, radical tweak to the timeline. Landon was always my best friend. But for me, he was my worst enemy growing up. Somewhere along the line of Lewis's, one of me came up with the bright idea of radically changing my psyche by leaving a young Landon the journal. He was instructed to torment me for most of the past decade."

"It's made Lewis bitter and less fun," said Mr. Gray, finally pulling himself up higher on Lewis's chest, "but it has also forced him to overcome more adversity in his life. It has hardened him."

"I've already figured out your plan little man," said Lewis. "You want me to write a warning to Landon in the journal he discovers as a kid. That way instead of being retroactively Erased out of this timeline he will suddenly be uno-reversed back into existence."

"Bingo!" exclaimed Mr. Gray. "Wildcard! And the only reason you even remember Landon to write this warning is because I've taken you out of your native time stream. So, you're welcome."

"Okay," said Lewis, "let's get to it, then. Lead the way."

Mr. Gray pointed down the street, away from Josie's house. "I should warn you, though," he said. "As soon as the shift happens, the Agares won't have left an hour ago. They will still be desperately searching this day to discover how Landon managed to slip through their net."

"My coil broke," said Lewis. "I won't be able to shoot back at them."

Mr. Gray's eyes flashed with excitement. "Well, then, it's finally time to see how well your childhood of adversity pays off!"

I got a real kick out of this part of the journey! Knowing more than everyone around you is a position of power us Parcae take very seriously, but that is not to say we don't have fun with it! I can say with the utmost certainty that Lewis (and all the Lewis's that came before) have single-handedly lived the most complicated life of any organism I've ever had the pleasure of working with. That journal and the notes that came before it have confused the Agares to no end by constantly shifting both the board and the game pieces right out from under them. It's a truly beautiful and convoluted-ly tragic tapestry Lewis, Landon, and all the others have managed to weave with my help. They say the real gifts in life are the friends we meet along the way, which I suppose would make the true tragedy all those who were permanently Erased and lost from memory. At least I'll always remember. Here's to you, Josh. Your sacrifice was forgotten, but if the Agares are defeated, it will not have been in vain.

Keep vigilant,

-Mr. Gray

CHAPTER

18

A Dreadful Surprise

"Water…" gasped the old man tied to a chair in Josie's garage. But of course it wasn't really an old man. It was a shapeshifting squid from another dimension.

Channie, having watched Josie and Lewis sneak away upon first arriving at the house, had been covering for them ever since. There was only so long, however, that claiming Josie was in the bathroom was going to work.

"Ooow, you want this?" asked Mrs. Davis as she twisted open a bottle of water, cracking its plastic seal with a pop. She took a big swig. "Ah! So refreshing! If only there was a squid around here that wanted to share it with me!"

"Please…" the shapeshifter gasped.

It was almost convincing as a human, despite its limited vocabulary, but Mrs. Davis and the kids knew better.

Channie diverted her eyes from the scene. She didn't want to have nightmares. Her gaze landed upon the fluorescent lightbulb at the center of the ceiling and stayed there until spots manifested across her vision.

Mr. Mays watched with his hands crossed in front of his chest. The creature was yet to out itself in front of him. He was becoming more and more disturbed by the possibility that everybody else was crazy and he was keeping a poor old kidnapped man tied up in his garage.

Channie sat down on the step that led up to the laundry room. The uncomfortable feeling of eyes on the back of her head drew her attention. She turned on the step and glanced through the open doors and down the dark hallway into the house.

She cursed the giant purple blotch left behind by the lightbulb. Before her eyes cleared, she saw motion—a head withdrawing behind the wall that concealed the stairs to the second story.

Josie?

Channie blinked several times, but the figure did not reemerge.

"Could you go check on Josie?" Mr. Mays directed the request to Channie.

That must have been her….

Channie nodded reluctantly. She climbed to her feet and wiped her damp palms on her jeans before setting off into the house. She was barely three steps beyond the laundry room when the garage door swung closed by itself.

Bang!

Channie jumped as it shut. A gust of wind blasted against the outside of the house, whistling through the eaves above.

She turned back around and continued towards the stairs, where she'd just seen the figure. The whole house was dark, apart from the limited natural light that made it this far back into the home. She felt along the wall as she walked, hoping for a light switch, but didn't find any.

"Josie? Are you in here?" Channie called out.

A door creaked somewhere up above on the second floor, but no one responded to her call.

"Josie? Lewis? Is that you guys?" Channie raised her voice slightly louder this time.

Still, there was no response.

She started up the stairs. "This isn't funny guys," she said. "Where are you?"

Two-thirds of the way up, Channie's eyes were elevated just high enough to see down the second floor hallway. A tall dark figure stood beyond an open door at the far end. It remained perfectly still, making Channie take pause.

She dropped down low to the stairs, out of sight. She was suddenly feeling stupid for having come to investigate all by herself. She lifted her head back up again slowly, locking her eyes once again on the shadowy shape. Her breath caught in her chest as she strained her eyes to make sense of what she was looking at in the darkness.

Channie shifted her hand slowly to her pocket, feeling for her butterfly knife. She was miffed to discover it missing.

"What are you doing?" asked Steph, suddenly at the bottom of the stairs behind her.

Channie dropped down again, spinning around as her heart nearly popped out of her chest.

Steph continued: "I saw Lewis and Josie run off before we came inside. And I saw you see them. No one's in here, so what are you doing?" she asked again.

Channie shushed her, with a finger pressed to her lips. "I thought I saw someone upstairs," she whispered. She gestured for Steph to climb up and look with her.

Steph approached hesitantly, rubbing her elbow nervously as she climbed the stairs below Channie.

Channie's eyes were finally starting to become better adjusted to the low light. She peered up above the plane of the second floor once more, searching for the figure in the darkness. The far doorway led into a bathroom. The shadow of a sink could be seen through the opening.

"What are we looking at?" whispered Steph upon reaching Channie's side. She leaned forward with Channie, both girls lying on their stomachs against the stairs.

The shadow Channie saw had been much taller than the sink. She rubbed her eyes, momentarily questioning the authenticity of her experience.

Thump.

Something heavy hit the ground, sounding from within a distant bedroom. Channie and Steph exchanged a look of concern.

"Maybe they have a cat…?" whispered Steph.

An inescapable sense of dread suddenly overcame Channie— a little bit of survival instinct kicking in. "Nope," she said. "I've changed my mind. I'm going back to the garage."

Steph scoffed. "You don't want to find out what made that noise?"

"After the day we've been having? No thank you." Channie edged away from the landing, pulling herself back up into a standing position with one hand on the railing. "You go be my guest."

As she turned back down the stairs, her eyes fell across an emaciated form inching around the corner at the bottom. It moved with slow, deliberate steps on all fours, moving ever closer on spindly limbs.

A hiss escaped its maw as it saw Channie see it.

Now I have to run up the stairs. People never survive in horror movies when they run up the stairs....

Channie couldn't get her legs to move. They were frozen up with terror. Locked in place. She was screaming at herself in her own head to move. At the same time, Steph was literally screaming out loud but looking in the opposite direction.

All at once the desperation of the situation suddenly sank in for Channie. The creature pounced forward up the stairs, scampering at its prey. Fear slapped Channie in the face hard enough to spin her around. Steph was trying to muffle her own scream with one hand while she pointed towards a second creature coming out of the bedroom.

Steph resisted Channie as she grabbed her arm, but she dragged Steph up the stairs despite the odds. The creature down the hall sprang out fully into the hallway—an old wrinkled man, proportioned like a pale naked spider. It scampered forward on all fours like the other one.

Channie turned sharply into the first room, whipping Steph in behind her. Steph tumbled past her into Josie's bedroom as Channie paused to slam the door shut behind them.

Wrinkled hands reached into the doorway. She grabbed the door with both hands and bashed it shut despite the fleshy resistance. Several white digits were severed, dropping to the ground, disjointed knuckles and all.

Channie clicked the lock shut as howls of pain erupted from the spider-people on the other side. The door shook with their pounding. It grew stronger until the hinges rattled and strained with their own groans. The growing pressure rumbled louder. The vibrations shook the fillings in Channie's teeth.

She stumbled backwards as the sensation grew unbearable. She didn't have time to turn away as the door exploded inward. The handle was left behind, broken off in the frame.

Channie fell backwards to the ground. There was nowhere to go. The slender monsters sprang at her angrily. They snapped at her ankles, gripping onto her before she could even attempt to scamper away. Their hands crushed her legs with such force that she whimpered in pain as they dragged her back out into the hallway.

She tried to grip onto the doorframe as she went by, but ended up with a fist full of severed fingers instead. She was yanked around the corner and slammed into the opposite wall. They pulled her into the back bedroom where there was more space for whatever they intended.

One kept hold of her legs while the other one jumped on top of her. It pinned her arms to her sides with its thighs and lowered its blood-slicked body against her slowly. She screamed as it dipped its angular face above hers. It looked eerily human, just twisted longer and brandishing a disgusting tangled beard that reeked worse than spoiled fungus in a garbage disposal.

It drooled into her face as it laughed a deep rumble of amusement. Channie's scream was ill timed. Its spittle tasted as bad as its beard smelled. Channie retched immodestly.

When the creature pulled back away from her face she was grateful, but only for a moment before it began its strike. Both monsters tore at her clothing, ripping away at her midriff until her flesh was exposed, and then they kept going, tearing at her as they chuckled. Their nails were stony, slicing into her. The elongated fingers slid right into her abdomen and stabbed and groped at her organs.

She felt herself being disemboweled, right up until the moment that she found herself screaming, laying on her back on the ground in the garage. Everyone was standing over her. There were no monsters in sight—other than the squid thrashing about, now in its true aquatic form, still tied to the chair, of course.

Everyone's faces held concerned expressions for Channie. She could hear herself screaming, but it took another moment before she could get herself to stop. She hadn't been asleep.

It was an attack!

All the terror of her experience was just as present as when those monsters' hands had been inside of her, tearing at her with malice and glee. It had all taken place inside her head, but it had *not* been her imagination. The only thing of which she was certain was that they were all in grave danger. In her heart she knew it true, the warning she delivered with dread to the group:

"The monsters know where we are!"

How dreadful! The group at Josie's house has no idea what they are up against. Safety in numbers doesn't really work when the enemy can put the terror directly into your mind. At least Channie is no sucker! The Dreadnaught knows where they are—it has seen inside Channie's head—the Agares will be coming for real now! I, of course, already know what's going to happen next, but you'll just have to wait and see if Channie's warning is enough to thwart the dark powers that are closing in.

Keep vigilant,

-Mr. Gray

Trick or Treat

Mr. Gray led Lewis and Josie to the time pocket in Yost Park. It was only a few blocks away in the green belt, spiderwebbed with trails. Lewis knew where he was going, generally, having been there before… in the future.

Josie was still trying to wrap her mind around the concept of Lewis's journal as they entered the park. Instructions from previous iterations of Lewis, refined by the ages—it was all pretty wild.

"So when you put new instructions into the journal, you change the past?" Josie asked as they stepped off the trail.

"Yup," said Lewis.

"And you've done this how many times?" she asked.

Lewis paused. "Well, I've never actually amended the journal myself, but possibly hundreds of past versions of me have sent back various instructions."

Mr. Gray laughed. "More like thousands of you, and that's just the current journal. You started with individual letters but it soon became unwieldy."

Josie nodded, soaking it all in. "Okay, but the part that's bothering me is that as soon you amend the journal, won't we cease to exist…? Like won't that replace us with a version that hasn't ever had to amend the journal because the journal will have always warned Landon not to be Erased and then we won't have needed to make this change? It will have always been there."

Lewis opened his mouth, but then closed it again as he contemplated the temporal ramifications of Josie's spot on logic. "Hey… you're right," he said. "Landon won't have been Erased and we'll just end up meeting him at his house earlier. We won't even think about going for the journal because it won't be needed."

Mr. Gray began laughing hysterically. The little imp slapped his knee as he cackled.

"What's so funny?" asked Lewis.

"Oh, nothing," said Mr. Gray. "Let's hurry now. We must stay on track. The pocket is just over there, under that root."

A thick tree root jutted out above the soil forming a hollow beneath. It was just wide enough for Lewis to crawl in with the upper half of his body. He dove in deep for the journal, screeched, then wiggled back out again backwards in a panic.

Mr. Gray cackled again, literally rolling on the ground in his laughter.

"Something's in there!" cried Lewis.

Earth shifted as a boy's head emerged from the hole. "Hello!" said the boy.

"Landon, I presume?" asked Josie.

The boy sneezed a puff of dusty dirt into the air. "The one and only," said Landon. "And you must be Josie. I've read all about you." He held up a tattered leather-bound journal.

"What are you doing in the time pocket?!" asked Lewis.

Landon smirked as he shimmied the rest of the way out from under the root. "Just following your instructions."

"I don't understand…" said Lewis. "You were Erased, and we haven't amended the journal yet."

Mr. Gray was absolutely losing his mind with laughter at this point. Josie suspected some sort of trick had been played on them.

"We went to your house," said Lewis. "Your dad said he didn't know who you were…."

Landon began laughing as well. "That wasn't my dad. That was my uncle. He's staying with us this week and he's a total jerk. No, I'm fine, look." He opened the journal to an entry they'd never needed to make. It detailed a plan for Landon to hide himself in the time pocket until retrieved.

"So we never had to write it, because we already did," Lewis was not amused.

"I brought all the stuff you asked me to bring," said Landon.

Lewis's mood shifted from annoyance to bubbling with curiosity.

Landon reached back into the time pocket and pulled out a backpack and a samurai sword. "Some of this wasn't easy to get my hands on, but I've had basically my whole life to prepare."

Lewis shook his head, smiling at his own ignorance. "What did I ask you to bring?"

"I'm not supposed to tell you," said Landon. "You do best when operating on pure instinct. But you'll need these." He unzipped his backpack, holding it close so that Lewis couldn't see inside. He retrieved a set of volunteer badges for the Taste of Edmonds festival that was going on that weekend at the civic center. "And you'll need this," he said to Josie as he handed her a strange nut, reminiscent of an acorn, with a hole drilled through it. A string was threaded through the hole, turning it into a necklace.

Josie looked at Landon quizzically as she accepted his offering.

"Put it on," he said, "it stops time from freezing for you, even in your native time stream. Basilisks."

Josie nodded in acknowledgment.

"It shouldn't sprout, but if it does, chuck it. As far as you can. And run."

Josie blinked several times.

"Okay, I gotta go," said Landon. "You two need to go back to Josie's house and convince the others to go to the Taste with Clark."

Lewis grabbed Landon's arm as he turned to go. "You've got to tell us more than that," he said. "I don't even know who Clark is."

"Oh, Clark is the shapeshifter," said Landon. "I figured you'd know that much since you refer to him by name in the journal."

"I wasn't allowed to read ahead," said Lewis.

Landon nodded slowly in understanding. "Ok, well, be nice to Clark, it's not his fault the Agares stole him from his universe." He looked contemplative for a moment. "The Agares are pulling out the big guns for today," he said, a concerned frown forming in his lips. "They have a Dreadnaught in town. It's our job to kill it."

Lewis's face turned stark white at the mention of the Dreadnaught.

"Yeah…" said Landon. "Basically the It clown on steroids."

Josie frowned. "I haven't seen that movie."

"It's a fear-inducing empath," said Lewis. "I've only read about them. They can manifest your worst fears."

"Delightful," said Josie.

"I'll prep the kill-zone," said Landon. "Get the others to the festival, and let's do this!"

Landon was way too pumped up for the encounter as far as Josie was concerned. "Wait," she said. "This Dreadnaught thing… the things it shows us, are they real or just in our heads?"

Landon shrugged. "I don't know, I've never met one." He swung his backpack over his shoulder and strapped his samurai sword to his belt. "Let's go, Gray," he said to the Parca. "Be safe out there," he said to Lewis and Josie. "I'll see you later when the time is right!"

Josie had no idea what the Dreadnaught might show her. Her biggest fears were more psychological than physical in nature. She hoped the encounter to be brief. She began to steel her mind to the possibilities.

That acorn looking thing is actually a Gobu nut. It grows on the same world that the Basilisks come from. The Basilisks freeze the native time stream, and only then can the Gobu nut grow, feeding off of the ambient energies inside of the Basilisks' vortex. Once the Gobu nut sprouts it can grow very large very fast, but it takes about a thousand years of frozen time for it to mature, so the risks of this aren't very high. By wearing the Gobu nut around ones neck on a necklace, the wearer is surrounded by the nut's aura and protected from the time freezing effect of the Basilisks. It's a very odd world that these things come from. Time is a real knot over there. The Basilisks were one of the first creatures that the Agares collected. The time freezing effect is fairly unique amongst species throughout the multi-verse, and the Agares often use them to inconspicuously Erase their enemies.

Keep vigilant,

-Mr. Gray

CHAPTER

20

Don't Listen to the Voices

Mr. Gray departed into the brush with Landon, leaving Josie and Lewis to find their own way out of Yost Park. They'd walked for several minutes through the woods, off trail, to get to the location of the time pocket. The hike back up the hilly terrain seemed steeper to Josie than when they first came down. It wasn't until Lewis started looking confused that Josie began to worry. They hadn't come across the path yet, or perhaps they had passed it already without realizing.

"The trail should be near," said Lewis. "It was just over the ridge."

The ground leveled out. They kept walking until they were both certain they must have overshot the path. Lewis paused and turned slowly in a full circle.

"I don't know how we got turned around..." he said. "I think the road is over that way." He pointed off to the left, into thicker brush.

They had to fight nature to cut their own path, pushing past branches with their bodies and stepping high to clear their feet over a layer of ivy. It was both slow and loud to trudge across the hillside. They walked back down the slope and up to another ridge, eventually coming across a narrow path that looked to have been formed by animals rather than humans.

"Do you think this will intersect with the main path?" asked Lewis.

Josie shrugged.

Lewis looked back and forth down the tiny winding animal trail. "I wonder what made this path…" he mused. "Which way should we go?"

Josie shook her head.

"Come on, you must have some idea of which way to go. Weren't you paying attention on the way in?"

Josie scowled at Lewis. "I know we met in a forest and all, but I grew up in the suburbs. You led *me* here! Weren't *you* paying attention?"

"I'm sorry," said Lewis, looking down at his feet. "I just feel stupid for getting turned around. I don't know how we missed the path…."

Josie huffed. "You know, I assumed you or Mr. Gray would be leading us back out."

Lewis wrung his hands together. "Yeah… Mr. Gray isn't always as helpful as it seems like he should be. He definitely knew we were going to get lost and didn't say anything." He pursed his lips in contemplation. "I'm just going to choose to believe everything is how it's supposed to be right now, otherwise he would have said something…."

"Everything in its own time," said Josie sarcastically.

"Exactly," said Lewis, missing her tone. "I'm sure we'll get back to the others precisely when we're meant to."

"We should go left," said Josie, making a decision simply to end the conversation.

Lewis craned his neck to look back down the trail for a moment. "Are you sure?"

Josie threw her hands up in exasperation. She started moving without Lewis. He hurried to catch up to her.

The landscape was deceptive. Little dips and rises hid the greater trend of the slope. Josie knew they'd walked downhill to get to the time pocket, but their current position was in a depression. Every direction was uphill. Her chosen heading was, in fact, random, but it was better than continuing to stand there just scratching their heads.

The trail meandered between the trees. Josie and Lewis continued along it, walking in a single-file line. It was easier to move through the bare patch in the ivy, but, unfortunately, after another twenty-five yards or so, the trail was abruptly consumed by the ivy again. They were left with nothing but their whims to carry them forward through the undergrowth.

Josie didn't notice anything was wrong when she heard the first distant knocks against the trees. She mistook the sounds as ordinary—perhaps just a couple of pine cones falling to the forest floor. It wasn't until the rest of the normal nature sounds receded away entirely that she knew she should have been paying more attention.

The breeze died down but the air felt charged, as if the woods had just inhaled and was now holding its breath. Josie paused, not wanting to disturb the silence.

Lewis nearly walked into the back of her. "What's wrong?" he asked.

Josie shushed him. They both stayed rooted in place within the crunchy ivy. Josie's pulse quickened.

Knock.

—A sudden loud click. The sound rang out from a nearby tree ahead, focusing her attention.

Lewis heard it as well. The dumb expression that appeared across his face did not instill any confidence.

"Josie!" came a distant cry. It sounded from the same direction as the knock, but from much farther out—maybe thirty or forty yards beyond where she could see.

"Did you hear…?" Lewis whispered behind her.

Josie silenced him with a glare.

"Josie!" yelled the distant voice again. "Where are you? Help! Help!"

The cries were desperate. They tugged at Josie. She wanted to rush forward… she recognized the voice but her mind couldn't place it. Only her fear stayed her heart. Something didn't feel right.

She sensed they were being watched….

A screech of tires on asphalt in the distance started a chain reaction of cascading sounds: A terrible crash—metal grinding against metal; glass shattering, worse than cracking bones to Josie's ears. It sounded like a thousand shovels being dragged across concrete at the same time, setting her senses abuzz.

When the crunching and groaning of the auditory carnage abated, all that remained was the sound of shards of raining glass tinkling to the ground like fairy dust. A bluster of wind followed, howling through the trees, carrying with it a chilly blast of mountain air.

And then the screaming began.

Terrible shrieks pierced the forest air; deep, pain-filled wails.

Josie knew it in an instant: It was the screams of her parents, mangled on the side of the mountain pass where they died. It didn't just sound *similar* to her parents dying screams, it sounded *exactly* like her parents dying screams.

Josie immediately began to question her perception of reality. *It can't be real....*

She turned towards Lewis. "Do you hear—?"

"The screaming?" he finished, nodding sharply, fear clear in his eyes.

The cries grew higher in pitch, becoming more shrill, like a teapot whistling in the woods.

"We should help them!" said Lewis. He wasn't thinking straight.

Josie realized they were already far too close to the voices. The cries of her parents couldn't possibly be authentic. Her parents were long dead. Five years gone and buried. Something was using the sounds to trigger her, and admittedly, it was working. Lewis could hear them too, though he had no idea of their terrible significance. Josie was being forced to mentally relive the moment of her parents' demise.

She nearly succumbed to the panic as her veins filled with ice, but her instincts forced her to stay alert. Something was trying to lure her, she realized.

The Dreadnaught…?

She scanned her eyes back and forth around where she remembered hearing the knock. At first she saw nothing, but then she spotted something amongst the lower foliage—elongated fingers gripping a branch.

It was an ambush.

They were dealing with a most unfortunate kind of evil—if she'd not taken pause and continued to follow the voices, it would already have been too late.

"We should go back now," whispered Josie. She kept her eyes locked on the hand as she took a slow, crunching step backwards into the ivy. Her shifting perspective took the menacing creature out of sight, but before it disappeared the fingers wiggled ever so slightly—whether as a sign of annoyance or simply the creature's way of saying hello, Josie didn't wish to find out.

"Shouldn't we be going towards the road?" Lewis asked, perplexed.

"That's exactly what it wants," Josie said harshly in a rushed whisper. She took another cautious step backwards. "Nothing we heard was real, but there *is* something out there. I saw it."

Lewis furrowed his brow, but followed Josie's lead.

Josie kept checking over her shoulder as they hastily made their way back towards the animal path. She kept her eyes peeled wide, praying not to see anything in pursuit. As soon as they reconnected with the animal path, Josie picked up the pace. Now that their feet were clear of the ivy, they could maintain a hopping jog within the clear patches of ground.

"Jooosssiee!" cried a high pitched voice, calling out from somewhere behind them. "Come back here, Josie! Come back!" A heckling screech pierced the stillness. "And Lewis!"

Lewis's jaw fell open as he looked back. "It knows my name…."

Josie flashed Lewis a disgruntled look. *It's been calling my name the whole time, but* now *he's concerned?*

Crunching ivy in the distance put additional fear in both of their steps. Something large was moving towards them, unconcerned about how loud it was being.

"Go, go, go!" cried Josie.

Lewis grabbed Josie's hand as they dashed through the trees. They ran as even-footed as they could along the animal trail, listening through their own heavy breaths to the footfalls steadily catching up behind them.

Suddenly, they burst through a fern and out onto the main path.

"Which way?!" cried Josie.

Lewis hesitated only momentarily before turning left, uphill. Behind them the crunching footsteps ceased at the edge of the trail. Their pursuer held back, remaining hidden in the brush, just out of sight.

They scampered up the hill, barely keeping their feet beneath them. The heckling voice continued its pursuit, calling out more to Lewis this time: "You won't escape your destiny, scrawny boy! You will die and rot, trapped in the cellar of that abandoned house!" It laughed out a taunting squeal of glee.

"Your Parca smells of burnt hair when he's Erased. Nothing will save you from the worms!"

Lewis and Josie's legs didn't stop pumping until long after they reached the paved drive that led from the city street to the community pool. The creature did not call out again, but they were too afraid to stop and breathe until they were entirely out of the park and partially down the road.

When they finally stopped running they were overlooking the bowl of Edmonds. The Taste of Edmonds festival was setting up for the day down below, about half a mile closer to the water. They could see the rooftops of half the downtown region from their vantage point at the top of the bowl-shaped drop-off to the coast.

Their eyes were immediately drawn upward in horror to a massive tear in the sky above the city. The aurora borealis swirled, forming an enormous conduit of spiraling energy. A huge flock of vampiric ghasts carrying all sorts of other creatures on their backs were emerging from the rift and diving down like darts to the rooftops below.

A middle aged woman walking her dog on the opposite side of the street paused to see what they were looking at. She took one glance before hastily continuing on her way.

"We should hurry back…" said Lewis.

The sparkling blue waterways of the Puget Sound reflected the yellow and green flashes of the ripped open sky.

"People are going to notice this…" said Josie.

Lewis frowned. "One would think," he said. "But I don't remember anything like this happening."

Josie squeezed onto Lewis's hand. Whatever it all meant for the timeline or their chances of success in the battle to come was beyond either of their abilities to assess.

The Agares horde descends. One never plans to be Erased, but I do hope more than a lingering scent of burnt hair is my ultimate legacy to the multi-verse. Bust out the marshmallows and chocolate for the fires to come if you have a high metabolism like me, otherwise, I hope you have good home insurance, because those ghasts will be taking off more than shingles! Fun fact: Not one person reported the hole in the sky that day to the police, not that they would have been able to do anything about it anyway.

Keep vigilant,

-Mr. Gray

CHAPTER

21

The Sky is Falling

Steph didn't miss the beeps and whirs of the hospital equipment, but the silence of the hospice room was even harder to bear. At least at the hospital there had been hope—she had clung to it like a life raft—the idea that there could still be some sort of miracle, that her father, Clark Bennett, might yet pull through. Steph's father's decline with aggressive lung cancer had been sharp and jarring to the whole family.

She was all cried out already. It had been less than a month since they got the bad news: The treatments had failed. The cancer won. Her father was a husk of his former self at this point. The chemotherapy, surgeries, and cancer combined to take away everything that made him her father. He was no longer present apart from small moments that were becoming less and less frequent.

Sleep or delirium was constant; food and water intake, rare. He was withering away and there was nothing Steph could do.

Nothing anyone could do. Steph listened to his unconscious, labored breathing, afraid it might stop at any moment.

The lack of awareness on her father's part was a blessing. The pain of being awake had become too much for him to bear. Everyone was simply waiting for him to die at this point, and Steph was *not* okay with any of it. The inevitability of his death put a pit in her stomach. Part of her was still holding on for a miracle, but the sympathetic expressions on all the nurses' faces hammered home the reality of the situation.

Steph was going to lose her dad. It hurt too much to even think the words.

Her mother, Lori, was asleep in the chair by her father's bedside, her hand clasped around his pale fingers. Everyone was exhausted by the emotional toll of the move to hospice.

Steph couldn't sleep, though she hadn't had more than a few hours of rest in the last several heart-wrenching days. She was seated in a chair across from her father's bed, with her feet up, legs bent, and her chin propped upon her knees. She didn't want to watch, but couldn't look away as her dad shuddered in his sleep and let out a wheeze. Time was short, but already there was no joy left.

"Stephanie…." A tiny whisper caught her attention.

She thought it was her mom at first, but she was still sleeping.

"Down here, Stephanie," whispered the voice again. It was coming from beneath her father's bed….

Steph's eyes grew wide. The fine hairs on the backs of her arms stood up as she lowered her gaze, but it was too dark to make out anything.   She strained her eyes, searching the shadow.

"May I speak with you for a moment?" the tiny voice squeaked.

"Am I asleep?" Steph whispered back, perplexed.

"Oh, no, no. You are very much aware."

Steph rubbed her eyes before focusing back on the shadow. This time, she could just barely make out a pair of eyes, reflecting back a little bit of light. The eyes were spaced at about the distance of a house cat's—a tiny head on a tiny body.

"My name is Nona," said the shadow.

Steph stared back at the eyes, too frightened to respond.

"I am a Fate," continued the creature within the darkness. "I know the future, but in order to get there, I need you to do something for me."

Steph narrowed her eyes. "You know the future?" she asked.

"Yes, my dear."

Her mind leapt to the only question that mattered. "What's going to happen to my dad?" she asked immediately.

"You already know the answer to that," said Nona. "He's going to die. Tonight."

Steph did know, but she wished she didn't. "Why are you here?" she asked.

"I already told you, I need you to do something for me… well, for your father, really. It's simple. I need you to give him some water."

Steph blinked several times, confused.

"Just pick up that glass over there and pour a little bit into his mouth."

Steph was hesitant, but she stood up from her seat and obediently approached the bedside. She picked up the glass of water from the side table and lifted it up to her father's slightly parted lips, all the while internally questioning her sanity.

"Good, good," said Nona. "Just pour a little in."

Her dad's emaciated body accepted the hydration, making small swallowing motions every couple of seconds.

"Keep going," said Nona.

Steph's wrist wobbled, pouring slightly faster than before. Her dad sputtered, still unconscious as he choked. Steph pulled away as the choking turned into convulsions. She backed up all the way to her chair.

Her mother woke up as her father's convulsions worsened. Tears streamed down Steph's cheeks as she searched for the eyes under the bed, but Nona was gone. Or perhaps the creature was never there to begin with. Regardless, the telling came true. Steph's father did not survive the night.

***

Steph had nearly forgotten all about her visit from the Parca. At the time, she'd chalked the experience up to stress and lack of sleep. All of it, especially her father's death had felt very surreal at the time. It still didn't feel real, but the loss had settled in more now, months later.

Standing in front of the shapeshifter in Josie's garage was bringing it all back to her now. The bright blue eyes of her father stared back at her.

"Please, water," it begged.

Steph glanced around the garage. Everyone else was fretting over Channie and her panic attack.

Steph wasn't prepared for this.

Seeing the shapeshifter look like her had been terrifying enough. Her father's strong arms appeared to be lashed excruciatingly tight with the rope Mr. Mays and Mrs. Davis had fashioned around the creature.

"Please, baby," cried her father's voice.

Steph felt her hands uncap a water bottle. Her feet brought her closer despite the danger. She was repeating her trauma, her body coached by her past actions.

"Yes, please… I'm so thirsty…." The shapeshifter opened its mouth in anticipation.

Steph felt compelled to oblige. As she poured the water into its desperate mouth, her mind flashed back to the voice under her father's hospice bed. She'd thought she'd made it up—that it was just her imagination running away with her—until recent events made her reassess everything.

She knew it wasn't her father sitting before her now, but she couldn't help but feel compassion for the shapeshifter's plight. It didn't stop gulping down the water until the bottle was completely empty. Steph backed away.

"Thank you," it said.

"Guys!" cried Rebecca from across the garage. "Something strange is going on outside, it looks like the sky is falling!" She pointed out through the tiny window at the top portion of the garage door and up into the air.

Steph glanced away from the shapeshifter for just a moment to observe the enormous rift in the sky above the town. She looked back again when a plop sounded. The shapeshifter was in its aquatic form again, slathered with fresh goo thanks to Steph's kindness. It had slipped free, and was already halfway across the garage before Steph could comprehend what was going on. It slithered and tumbled across the floor with a sudden burst of speed as it made its escape. It flopped through the open door into the house and was out of sight a moment later.

Steph peered around the garage again. No one else had noticed. They were all still staring out the window at the hole in the sky.

"Things are flying through!" exclaimed Mr. Mays.

"We need to get out of here now!" cried Channie. "They know where we are!"

Mrs. Davis didn't need to be told twice. She turned around first to see the shapeshifter missing and didn't hesitate a moment more before running over to the garage door switch and hitting it.

The belt sprang into action, lifting the door. It had risen less than a foot when banging on the outside startled everyone. Lewis and Josie came rolling under a moment later.

"Shut the garage!" yelled Lewis.

Mrs. Davis ignored the warning. Instead, she grabbed Channie and her purse and ducked out while the door was still only halfway up. She was in full-on panic mode as she shoved Channie into the car and ran around to get into the driver's seat.

Steph stepped outside, her eyes drawn to the tear in the sky. Swirling clouds poured through the opening into an otherwise clear afternoon. The churning atmospheres soon masked the opening in the universe. Dozens of dark winged figures continued to burst through the mist, descending all across the city.

Mrs. Davis didn't wait for anyone else to join them. She started her car's engine and peeled out of the driveway. She didn't make it very far, however, before a ghast crashed against the hood. A moment later, the car was crumpled against a utility pole on the other side of the street.

It all happened so suddenly that Steph didn't have time to process much as Mr. Mays pushed past her, a hunting rifle already raised in his arms.

The ghast clucked and cackled as it bashed against the car's windshield, shattering it and knocking it inwards. Channie screamed from within. Mrs. Davis was unconscious, knocked out by the airbag deployment.

Bang!

A shot rang out—Mr. Mays lowered his rifle from his shoulder as the ghast collapsed dead.

Steph was dazed by the sound of the gunshot. The world was moving too quickly for her to fully process everything that was happening. Her mind was hung-up on the realization that her actions had been the catalyst to it all. The fact that her trauma had informed and guided her actions was not lost on her either.

Everyone else followed Mr. Mays as he ran over to the car. Together they dragged Mrs. Davis, still unconscious, from the driver's seat and back across the street to the house. A wound on Mrs. Davis's head was bleeding heavily. Together, Lewis and Mr. Mays managed to heft her into the backseat of Mr. Mays' car.

"I need to get her to the hospital," said Mr Mays. "But my car isn't big enough for all of us."

"We need to get to the Taste of Edmonds and kill something called a Dreadnaught," said Josie.

"Well that doesn't sound very safe," said Mr. Mays with a frown.

"It's the only way any of us are surviving," said Lewis.

"We should split up," said Channie. "I know that's a sin in the movies, but I've seen what the Dreadnaught can do…. It already knows we're here. We all just need to get out of here!"

"Actually, we are all supposed to go at the festival," said Lewis. "That's what Landon said."

"Well, I don't know Landon," said Channie, "so I'm going with my mom to the hospital."

Lewis opened his mouth to argue but Josie preempted him. "It's okay, go to the hospital, but please come meet us downtown as soon as you can," she said. "Lewis's friend said he would meet us later, so we should have some time, but we are going to need everyone's help to kill this thing."

Channie shook her head. "You don't know what it can do to you. You don't want to get anywhere near that thing. It gets in your head…."

"If we don't kill it, it won't stop hunting *all* of us until each and every one of us is dead," said Lewis bluntly.

"I guess I do kind of trust you, boy I met in the woods yesterday," Channie said sassily.

Lewis squinted, unsure if she was being sarcastic.

"You better take this thing serious," said Channie. "It'll show you such terrible stuff…."

"What part of me saying 'it will kill us all' sounded like I was planning on screwing around?" asked Lewis.

"Fair enough," said Channie. "I guess we'll see you later then…."

Mr. Mays gave Josie a tight hug. "Be careful out there," he said. He placed his rifle into her arms. "You know how to use this."

Josie nodded, her eyes glistening with moisture.

Steph allowed herself to be ushered into the car alongside Channie—temporarily splitting up the group. Her body took her through the motions, her mind still reeling from seeing the shapeshifter take her father's form. Steph felt in her gut that she had been manipulated by both the shapeshifter and the Parca, Nona, in the past, though she didn't yet know the ramifications of her actions.

Eyes watched them from the rooftop as they departed for the hospital. Steph thought she saw herself poised up there while glancing at the rear view mirror for a moment, but by the time she turned around, the figure was gone.

Things are moving along quickly! The children aren't taking the time to contemplate all their decisions, but the path that is forming is still holding to my expectations. There are some interesting points in this portion of the journey that shouldn't be overlooked: Stephanie's past has come back to haunt her, and her dead father WHOSE NAME IS CLARK is being impersonated by the shapeshifter, also named Clark. Hint: This is not a coincidence and has never failed to color Steph's interactions with the shapeshifter going forward. Also of interest, for those of you who are not yet familiar with the nuances of Lewis's history with us Parcae, or if you just need a refresher, Nona, the Parca under the hospice bed, is one of our great leaders. She is one of The Council of Three, the highest position public servant in the multi-verse. Her presence in Steph's life is quite a gift, for she rarely manipulates so directly. The Council of Three consists of Nona, Decuma, and Morta. They are all so famous that even you mortals have made up some stories about them that have become embedded across numerous Earth cultures. Those three are the first thought of when Fates are brought up in cultured conversation for a reason. I'm a big fan of their work if that isn't obvious. I'm sorry, I don't mean to rant, but they really are just on top of their game when it comes to orchestrating the on-goings of the multi-verse. The web those ladies weave is the most glorious tapestry to ever exist.

* Keep vigilant,*
-Mr. Gray

CHAPTER

22

Clark (the shapeshifter)

"Don't look now," said Rebecca, "but *Steph's* on the roof."

Josie and Lewis looked up towards the roof simultaneously. They all knew it wasn't really Steph. The shapeshifter, posing as Steph, retracted its head out of sight.

"I told you *not* to look," said Rebecca, wrinkling her nose. The shapeshifter had a peculiar scent to the girl stricken with vampirism—the smell had drawn her attention to the roof. Nobody else seemed to notice the sickly sweet, metallic aroma on the air. It was something akin to raw tomato paste in Rebecca's mind. All of her senses had been wonky since recovering from her ghast bites and contracting the fabled disease.

A metabolic change had started inside of her. She was becoming something else—something more than human. Mr. Gray had downplayed the severity of her condition, but the implications were worrisome. The rays of the sun felt particularly repressive today, as if she were frying under a heat lamp.

The changes to her senses weren't all bad, though. On top of being able to smell the shapeshifter, she could also tell that it wasn't human just from looking at its attempt at a human face. In every form the creature had taken in front of Rebecca (that of several old men, and Steph) she felt like she was looking at a dog in human skin for how obviously wrong it was. It was something about the width of the head being slightly too narrow, but also in the ratios of its eye placement. She couldn't quite explain it, but to her it was glaringly obvious. Nobody else seemed to notice the discrepancies.

Lewis and Josie shared a knowing look. Neither one of them appeared to be particularly worried about the presence of their shape-shifting stalker above.

"What gives?" asked Rebecca.

Lewis shook his head. "Don't worry about it, he will be an ally soon. His name is Clark."

Rebecca narrowed her eyes. "How could you possibly know that…?"

Lewis and Josie shared another silent look. Their non-verbal communication game was on point. Lewis shook his head. Josie raised an eyebrow. Then Lewis sighed. He begrudgingly delved into the explanation of his time-traveling journal.

Rebecca stared at him incredulously as she mulled the concept over in his mind. "So you wrote a diary, and now it has come back in time to you through a time pocket and it predicts the future," she repeated back her understanding of the situation.

"More or less, but it's a journal, not a diary," Lewis said defensively.

Rebecca laughed. "No, it's okay, I think it's cute when a boy writes down his feelings."

"It's really not like that," said Lewis.

Rebecca nodded, amused by how easily flustered Lewis had become. Rebecca wasn't usually so confident around boys, not enough to tease them anyway, and certainly not around older boys like Lewis. A daring streak was growing inside of her. It felt foreign to her typical temperament, which was usually much more reserved. Her mind raced, almost like a caffeine buzz. She couldn't help but ponder if the shift inside her was symptomatic of her vampirism.

Rebecca wasn't teasing Lewis because of any attraction to him—it was actually quite the opposite. She was asserting her dominance. She couldn't quite explain it, but she sensed a weakness within Lewis. He seemed like a nice enough guy and all, however, he reeked of fear.

The smell was sweet to her, like honey-glazed ham. It's not that she wanted to bite him and drink all of his blood—she had been able to control herself better since receiving an elixir from Mr. Gray early that morning—it's just that the thought of biting Lewis and drinking all of his blood did cross her mind at an alarmingly unhealthy rate. The smell of fear seeped out of his every pour with his sweat. He was prey. And as prey, he was simply unattractive to her. It was definitely the vampirism leading the feelings as she thought about it more, but she couldn't help how she felt. He was as attractive to her as a pig or chicken.

"Stop staring at me like that..." said Lewis.

Rebecca diverted her eyes. She realized her mouth was watering. She'd been gazing at Lewis like he was a soup dumpling. She could sense his elevated blood pressure pulsing through his veins. "Sorry," said Rebecca. She didn't share her feelings. She didn't want to alarm anyone. She could control the cravings.

Lewis continued to watch Rebecca with a small frown on his face.

"What should we do about Clark?" asked Josie, thankfully turning the conversation away from the awkward moment.

Lewis pursed his lips. "Clark will lead us to the Dreadnaught, but we have to convince him to help us first.

"So we need to catch him again so that we can talk to him," said Rebecca. She knew what needed to be done, and surprisingly she didn't feel any reservations about going after the shapeshifter.

A maple tree in Josie's front yard had a wide branch that led perfectly to the lower roof line above the front porch. Rebecca walked over beneath the branch and jumped as high as she could, easily latching onto it with her arms. She swung her legs up, dangling upside down like a bat for a moment before pulling herself all the way up. Her scrawny muscles felt supercharged. She hopped up and ran the length of the branch with precise balance and agility.

It felt good to move. She hadn't realized how much she'd been holding back by pretending to be ordinary.

She glanced back down at Lewis and Josie. They looked dumbfounded as she leapt spryly from the branch onto the roof.

The shapeshifter, still masquerading as Steph, picked its head up again at the sound of the thud as Rebecca landed on the roof like a gymnast. The shock on its face was laughable as the stalker became the stalked.

Rebecca ran up the steep roof, releasing a war cry as she dove headfirst at the unsuspecting creature. Tentacles shot out and wrapped around her as they bounced once together against the roof and then fell roughly to the ground behind the house.

The vampirism made Rebecca stronger than ever as she sat up on top of the shapeshifter and held it by the throat. "Don't struggle," she said.

Josie and Lewis came running around the house into the backyard.

The shapeshifter's tentacles went limp as Rebecca raised a threatening fist above its slightly narrow Steph-face. It slowly retracted its extra appendages back into its human disguise—a show of submission. Rebecca lowered her hand again as Lewis joined her at the creature's side.

"Hello," said Lewis, addressing the shapeshifter. "I don't know your whole story, or even if you can fully understand me, but I do know you were taken by the Agares against your will."

The shapeshifter stared back at Lewis blankly.

"I know you are going to go by the name Clark, eventually," continued Lewis. "And that you are going to be our friend."

"Fffur," said Clark, the sound escaping like a hiss.

"Friend," repeated Lewis. "We are friends."

"Frieends," said Clark, sounding like a German exchange student. His eyes—Steph's eyes—bulged as he made an awkward grimace.

"Yeah, that's right," said Lewis, chuckling.

Rebecca let go of Clark's throat and sat back slightly. He didn't struggle. His eyes shifted between the children.

"*Ar gahtoa du vary se'lina happo,*" said Clark. He made a cluck sound like a chicken. "*Du gardo hano.*"

"What?" asked Lewis.

"Frieends ride. Get low," said Clark. "Low low low. With the furr!"

"Ah, yeah," said Lewis. "The song, from the car. You like music, don't you, Clark?"

Clark giggled like Steph. It was creepy.

"I know where we can listen to some more music," said Lewis. "There's a band playing at the Taste of Edmonds. You can hear it, can't you?"

The distant drone of live rock music sounded from across town at the festival. Rebecca wondered if anyone else other than them had even noticed the tear in the sky. Life was going on as normal down below. The hole was still up there, but a billowy cloud completely hid the opening in the universe at this point. The mist was falling down and settling across the town; a peculiar warm fog.

"We need to go to the music," continued Lewis. "The Dreadnaught is down there somewhere, and if you help us kill it, we can all be free of the Agares."

Clark's face drooped into a frown. "Agares bad," he said.

"Yes," said Lewis. "Agares very bad."

"Dreadnaught very very bad," said Clark.

Lewis nodded. "You lead us to it, we kill it, then we are all free."

"Free," said Clark. "For music?"

"Yes, we can listen to all the music you want, after you lead us to the Dreadnaught."

Clark nodded in agreement. "The Dreadnaught will devour you. There is no hope."

Josie and Rebecca shared a look of concern.

"We have to do it," insisted Lewis. "It's the only way. We just need you to lead us there."

"I will help," said Clark. "I'm supposed to bring you to them. They will reward me.... You should run, leave this universe behind."

"I can't do that," said Lewis.

"I will not enjoy your deaths. They will," Clark said flatly.

Rebecca stood up, getting off of the shapeshifter entirely. Clark remained in Steph's image as he looked up at her.

"She is scary," said Clark, pointing at Rebecca.

More savoy sweet fear wafted from Lewis's pores as his eyes darted over to Rebecca. Josie's hand subconsciously went to her neck at the same time. Only a faint scar remained where Rebecca bit her. Josie wasn't afraid of Rebecca, but she was wary.

"The Dreadnaught hungers for terror, just like her," said Clark.

Rebecca voiced a shrill bark at Clark. "*Arp!*"

Everyone flinched.

They should *be scared me!* thought Rebecca. *I'm feeling better than ever!* She rolled her eyes at their frowns. "Scared of a little girl? Whatever. Let's go kill this Dreadnaught." Fierce intensity burned behind her eyes. The vampirism had changed her, but she didn't care. She relished in her growing strength.

Okay, okay, I know what you're all thinking.... I may have underplayed the severity of little Rebecca's affliction. Vampires in real life aren't quite like the ones on TV! Rebecca is going through a metamorphosis most interesting. I've seen her life play out in many different ways across the ages, but none are quite as spectacular as Vampire Becca. A scrawny thirteen-year-old scampering up a tree, over the roof, and linebacker tackling a squid person? Ridiculous! But believe me when I tell you, this kid is just getting started! Take that, ordinary life!
Keep vigilant,
-Mr. Gray

CHAPTER

23

Inhospitable

After arriving at the emergency entrance to the hospital, Mr. Mays left Steph and Channie in an empty waiting room while he accompanied a still delirious Mrs. Davis on her way to get her head scanned.

Steph couldn't sit still. She had spent far too many hours in waiting rooms during her father's decline with cancer. Her fidgeting toes caused a tap in her foot against the linoleum floor. Channie shot her a dirty look to get her to stop making the noise. Steph frowned. "I'm going to find a vending machine," she said as she hopped up to her feet.

"You have money?" asked Channie.

Steph's frown deepened. "I was just gunna ask a nice nurse or doctor to pay for me."

"That's some next level privilege right there," said Channie.

Steph glared back at her indignantly. "I'm sure someone would buy you something too, even if you are a bitch."

Channie's eyes bulged. "Oh, is that so? Well, for your information, I don't need to beg for dollars like a stanky hoe—I got my mom's purse." She held up the dark blue on-brand clutch like it proved something. "You comin' up in here callin' me names? Who even invited you here with us?"

Steph scoffed. Her temper had gotten the better of her. "Technically I didn't say you were a bitch, just that people would still buy you stuff regardless," she said, backtracking. "And you started it, calling me privileged."

"You *are* privileged," said Channie.

"You don't know anything about my life," spat Steph.

Channie rolled her eyes. "You and your perfect blonde hair and blue eyes think you know something about struggle? Tell me, how many nights have you spent living out of a car down on that farm of yours?"

Steph, admittedly, had never been homeless, but she was still dealing with a profound loss. The subject of her father was not something she was willing to talk about with anyone. Especially not with Channie. She felt her face beginning to grow hot with a combination of anger and embarrassment. She turned on her heel and stormed off before it could get any worse.

Tears welled up in her eyes immediately. She didn't want Channie to see her cry. She put as much distance as she could between them. She didn't stop moving until she reached a bank of elevators. The cafeteria was one floor up, so she hit the 'up' button and attempted to settle her emotions while she waited.

A ding sounded as the elevator arrived. Steph rubbed her eyes with the back of her sleeve as she stepped in. She hit the button for the cafeteria, but the light inside the button didn't stay on as the elevator started moving downwards instead.

Steph hit the cafeteria button repeatedly, but the elevator refused her input, continuing down below ground level despite a lack of any basement button options on the panel.

The lift bumped to a jarring stop.

An uneasy feeling gripped ahold of Steph's stomach.

The back side of the elevator slid open revealing a dark hallway behind her. She didn't notice at first, not realizing that the elevator could open on both sides. After slamming the cafeteria button several more times in despair, a sharp bang like a mop handle hitting the floor rang out from down the hallway behind her.

Steph jumped at the sound, turning around in fright. Construction signs partially blocked the dim corridor. It was Saturday—no one was around, but something had made the bang. She tried the 'close door' button, but it didn't do anything.

A sign on the wall opposite the elevator opening labeled Steph's current location as the morgue. The elevator wasn't supposed to come here without a keycard presented by hospital staff. After the day she was having, Steph didn't want anything to do with a creepy place like this.

The lights are literally flickering down here….

Another bang sounded in the distance—a slammed door this time.

Steph stayed on the elevator, trying the buttons again and again for every floor in turn. The doors stayed open. None of the button presses worked. The lights in the elevator began to flicker on and off along with the rest of the basement lights.

She decided to try a different elevator.

As soon as she stepped out, the door closed behind her. She searched for an 'up' button to hit, but found it required an ID card to access the elevators on this floor. The lights in the hallway flickered again. It seemed like the whole basement was having some sort of electrical disturbance.

Steph sighed. It was just one thing after another.

She began searching for some stairs, but the stairwell that resided next to the elevator bank on the first floor didn't extend into the basement.

The signs on the wall indicated that the morgue was to the left, and the radiology department was to the right. Both directions were only sporadically lit. Steph wasn't about to go anywhere near the morgue. She turned right and headed towards what would have been the radiology department if renovations hadn't shut down the whole floor. Channie's mom had been brought up to the fifth floor for her head scan instead.

Hospitals always creeped Steph out—she associated them with death—and that was when they were still full of people! She walked as quietly as she could through the empty basement searching for a way back up.

The magnetic hums and banging of an active MRI machine could be heard behind a closed door. Steph pushed the door open, hoping to find some hospital staff to help her. Inside was an empty observation room. A pane of glass separated the room filled with monitors from the large tube of the MRI machine.

She couldn't see inside the machine from her angle, but bursts of light flashed eerily from the powered-up machine, coinciding with the flickering hallway lights.

I don't think it's supposed to be doing that....

No one was around as the imaging equipment whirred and clicked.

A strange shape on one of the monitors caught Steph's attention. She narrowed her eyes as she took in the strange twisted form.

The door to the observation room banged shut as a shift in airflow occurred out in the hallway. It startled Steph, but it wasn't until the shape on the screen began to uncoil that her heart really started racing.

Whatever was in the tube was certainly not human. It unfolded slowly like a contortionist out of a suitcase. Steph backed away from the window. A pale hand extended out from the opening of the MRI tube. Jagged nails gripped the side of the machine as the creature began to pull itself free.

Steph didn't wait around.

She threw open the door and sprinted out into the hallway, back towards the elevators. Glass shattered behind her as whatever had been in the tube smashed through into the observation room. Steph bounded past the closed elevators in the only direction available to her: Towards the morgue.

She dared only a single glance behind her as the hallway took an abrupt left turn. A ceiling-tall corpse-white figure slumped out of the observation room. It had to hunch its naked body to fit through the doorway. Before Steph's attention returned to what lay ahead, the lanky monster dropped its humanoid form down to all fours and pounced after her like an alien wolf chasing a rabbit.

Steph didn't immediately realize she was shrieking with terror. She only became aware of her screams when she had to stop to take a breath. She ceased her cries immediately, but already was on the verge of panting for air. She needed to hide somewhere, and fast! There would be no out-running the horrific entity at her back.

The hallway felt more like a tunnel. A door-less stretch plunged her into shadow. The lighting was almost entirely burned out or missing apart from a single flickering halogen tube directly above the opening to the morgue. There was nowhere else to go.

The galloping stride of the naked horror behind her put a frantic pace to her own sprint. The slaps of her shoes against the linoleum floor rang out as a loud chorus of confusion. She rushed into the morgue, spotted an empty corpse drawer, jumped up and shuffled in feet first without hesitation. Several of the other drawers that covered the wall were also in various open positions allowing minimal light into the refrigerated compartment behind the wall. She closed the metal hatch in front of her slab.

There was an occupied body bag on the slab to her left.

None of these hatches should have been left open….

Steph eyed the bulging bag anxiously as she tried to get her heavy breathing under better control. The black plastic crinkled slightly in the disturbed air. The hatch one slab beyond the body bag was halfway open. The light changed in the compartment as the slender monstrosity pursuing her moved silently across the morgue outside, bypassing the corpse storage.

Steph held her breath, attempting to be completely silent, but more rustling sounds emanated from the body bag beside her. Her attention and concern returned to the black plastic at once. She had not disturbed the bag this time, but it continued to crinkle and shift as if its inhabitant was not quite yet dead.

The bag suddenly lurched upright, bending into an L-shape as the body inside sat up. Steph covered her mouth with her hands, stifling her panicked gasps. The open hatches took on a terrible new explanation in Steph's mind: The corpses had risen from the dead and left the hatches open as they crawled out!

The zipper on the body bag began a shift steadily open.

A clatter of jostled equipment sounded from deeper in the morgue offices as the slender monster continued its search for her. Steph shoved open the hatch and used both arms to pull her whole slab out. The metal drawer clanged as it fully extended.

Steph threw herself from the slab. She landed hard on her hands and feet simultaneously. A screech from the morgue offices told her the tall monster was coming for her again.

She scampered up to her feet and sprinted back down the dark hallway in a pure panic.

She had nowhere to go.

She turned the corner as the monster reached the hallway and once again dropped down to all-fours to mount its pursuit.

Steph was moving too fast. She skidded into the wall at the turn, barely managing to keep up her pace as she pushed onward. She soared down the hallway on desperate legs towards the elevator bank.

She had a split second to make a decision when she realized one of the elevators was waiting on her floor, doors open. If the buttons still weren't working, she would be a sitting duck, but venturing back into the abandoned radiology department was hardly a better option.

She pivoted at the opening, swinging herself inside, and then slammed the 'ground floor' and 'close door' buttons simultaneously with the palm of her hand. The light inside the 'ground floor' button stayed lit this time.

She could hear the galloping slaps of the monster's hands and feet growing imminently closer. For a moment before the doors began to slide shut, she thought she had made the wrong decision by getting on the elevator. The creature reached the doors while they were only inches apart. Its pale face snarled at her through the remaining crack. Its eyes were black dots, fixated on her. Its angular face wasn't human, but its anger was still obvious to Steph.

The doors finished closing and the elevator began its slow rise back out of the depths of despair.

Close call on that one, don't ya think? There was a bit too much left up to chance for poor little Steph, at least for my personal comfort. It has always been about a 50/50 chances that the elevator doors close in time to save her from that nasty Agares during previous attempts at this journey. On timelines where Steph doesn't make it, the Agares rips her apart... very gruesome. He doesn't Erase her like they usually try to do because his coil was fried by the MRI machine's extreme magnetism. It sucked it right off his arm and into the tube! That's why that dope was in there to begin with, all twisted up like that—he was trying to pry it from the wall of the MRI machine! The MRI takes out the coil every time, like clockwork. I'll give you one guess as to who turned it on. The sound of the mop handle hitting the floor that Steph thought she heard when she first reached the basement was actually the sound of my portal disintegrating upon my departure. You're welcome. When Steph doesn't make it, she doesn't end up saving Jerry, and without Jerry, the future has a little less goat in it. Never underestimate the power of the randomness of a goat for throwing a wrench in the works of the Agares contingent.

Keep vigilant,
-Mr. Gray

CHAPTER

24

Through the Mist

Billowing clouds emerged from the hole in the sky and descended across the suburb in a dense mist. The unnatural fog drifted down concealing the tops of the nearby houses. The city center was directly below the hidden hole high above. The closer Josie's party got to the Taste of Edmonds festival, the thicker the clouds became.

The air felt unseasonably warm as the otherworldly atmosphere filled Josie's lungs. Breathing in the unfamiliar climate made her uncomfortable. There was no escaping the mist. The heat of it reminded her of metro bus exhaust. She tried to avoid inhaling as a particularly heavy arm of fog rolled across her. The wave crashed down the street, looking like an avalanche. It whipped against her face like hot smoke as it enveloped her.

"This is freaky," said Rebecca as she ran her fingers through the thick swirls.

Lewis pulled his shirt up over his face. If the air was harmful to breath, it was already far too late.

Clark, still mimicking Steph, walked beside Rebecca. Both were watching the sky for threats, though there would be little warning of an attack with the visibility as minimal as it was. The two of them had come to a silent understanding, despite Clark's fear of the girl with Vampirism.

Josie watched curiously as they each sniffed at the air. Their reactions to the fog were similar, each of their facial expressions softening, as if put to ease by the strange atmosphere.

The comfort in Rebecca's steps was disconcerting to Josie. Because of the Vampirism, Rebecca seemed to have more in common with the shape shifting squid than with the other humans around her.

Josie couldn't help but wonder what the alien disease might be doing inside Rebecca's mind. She certainly hadn't been acting herself. Josie briefly recalled the lifecycle of the *Ophiocordyceps unilateralis* fungus. She'd been fascinated when learning about it one evening while browsing random wiki's. It had one goal, and that was to spread itself far and wide. To achieve its goal, it would infect foraging ants, where it would then take over the ants' minds and force them to act against their survival instincts. The infected ants would walk to the tips of blades of grass and wait to be eaten by birds, carrying the fungus onward.

She had no idea what Vampirism might do. It wasn't even from their universe. The physical possibilities were not comforting to consider.

Suddenly, Rebecca stiffened. Her neck swiveled to look down a cross street. She gestured for everyone to get low behind a nearby parked car.

"What is it?" whispered Lewis as he ducked down beside her.

Rebecca put her finger to her lips.

Not a moment later, a figure the size of a large buck stepped silently into view within the mist.

A giant ghast!

Its slick black form was unmistakable. It easily had five times the mass of the dog-sized variety Josie had seen back at camp. Its clawed appendages almost looked like human hands. With slender limbs like a deer and giant bat wings tucked to its side, it was a true picture of horror.

The foul creature paused in its stride and craned its neck, scanning the road ahead. Its eyes were placed on opposite sides of its skull like a raptor.

It paused while looking in their direction. After a moment of stillness, its jaw opened and it cried out with the breathy sob of a child.

Josie shuddered.

It turned its head the opposite direction and cried out again. "Halp meh!" it croaked. "Halp me-mommy!"

A wave of terror shot through Josie. The almost parrot-like cadence struck a nerve with her.

It can speak....

She didn't want to know how it had learned those words.

Wild energy tugged at her muscles, but she forced herself to remain perfectly still. She gripped her grandfather's rifle tight at her side. She didn't want to waste bullets she might need for the Dreadnaught. She was also concerned a single shot wouldn't be enough to put down the giant ghast. Plus there was no telling how many more were within earshot.

It turned sharply and walked off with gentle steps into the billows of fog.

Rebecca held up her fist and waited for another fifteen seconds before gesturing that they should all continue past the intersection at a fast clip. Everyone was happy to submit to Rebecca's leadership. Her heightened senses and new-found physical aptitude made her the obvious choice to steer the group through the unknown threats ahead.

Their trajectory was mostly downhill as they made their way through the bowl of Edmonds to the Taste. The festival was underway this weekend at the civic center. Up until recently, they had been able to hear a band playing over the loud speakers in the distance, but the sound had ceased about half a mile back when the fog fully descended. After seeing the ghast, Josie feared the worst.

A dense cloud stood eerily still in front of them about half a block ahead. It loomed over them like an impenetrable wall, too thick to see anything beyond. They approached slowly, listening for anything in the unnatural stillness. All remained silent. A strange sense settled across Josie—evil, waiting for them. The Dreadnaught was in there.

It felt like the world was holding its breath at the center of town. As they approached the fog bank, a quality of the air changed. It felt somehow heavier, as if more dense. Josie's movements were ever so slightly slowed, a fraction more energy required for every step forward. It was like they were moving through a fluid rather than just air.

Josie could almost assume the sensation was just in her head, but the lack of any air movement within the fog bank spoke to a supernatural origin. Lewis grabbed ahold of her hand as they stepped into the cloud. They became fully engulfed by the atmosphere pouring in through the unseen hole above. Josie took several tentative breaths, but the air still went down smooth despite it being weirdly hot and moist.

Rebecca breathed in deeply beside her. Josie could just barely see her through the dense fog. She did have to admit, the air felt fresher than what they had been breathing on the other side of the fog bank.

"Time frozen here," said Clark, invisible on the other side of Rebecca.

Lewis swore under his breath. "It's Basilisks," he said. "No wonder the band stopped. This is going to complicate things."

Josie's hand pulled free of Lewis's and went to the nut dangling from the necklace Landon had given her. It felt warm to the touch. It was the only reason she wasn't frozen. Lewis and the shapeshifter were both out of their native time streams, making them immune to the basilisk's abilities.

Josie glanced back towards Rebecca, but she was no longer beside her. She turned back, and had to take several steps before she could see the girl within the fog. Rebecca was frozen in place, one leg hanging awkwardly in the air, mid-stride. Rebecca and her new abilities had been their best chance at defeating the Dreadnaught, but now, she would not be able to go any farther with them on their mission.

"Josie!" came Lewis's nearby call. His voice rang out hollow, the direction unclear within the opaque cloud.

A nearby child's scream pierced the eerily still air.

Definitely another ghast.

Smartly, Lewis did not call out again.

Josie couldn't leave Rebecca behind, helplessly frozen in place. If anything else came by, she would be a sitting duck. She quickly put down her grandfather's rifle and grabbed ahold of Rebecca's arms. She intended to drag her off the sidewalk and into the bushes, but just as she started pulling, a figure burst into her vision.

Josie fell back, leaving Rebecca lying on the pavement. It took her a moment of fright to recognize Clark standing before her, still disguised as Steph.

A short giggle sounded down the block.

"I hide her, you must help Lewis," said Clark.

Josie nodded in understanding. She snatched the rifle back up as she climbed to her feet. She didn't know if she could fully trust the shapeshifter, but she didn't have any other choice. She held the rifle high in her arms as she crept quietly in the direction she hoped to find Lewis.

Things are already falling apart for our would-be heroes. The disadvantages just keep stacking up! They were supposed to be using Clark as a guide, but now everyone's all split up, and Vampire Becca is sidelined by a simple time vortex. Not their best moments here. Josie may get a sense of foreboding over the Dreadnaught waiting for them, but for me, the challenge I know to be ahead puts butterflies in my stomach. The outcome is balanced on a knife's edge, probability-wise anyway. Of course, me being a master of probability, the more unlikely the happenstance, the more fun it is to throw in the faces of the Agares! Unfortunately, the alternative to a victory here is total annihilation, with absolutely no middle ground whatsoever. Either the gang figures out how to come together to defeat the master of nightmares, or else terror reigns supreme and before you know it the Agares will have Erased every single one of these important children. Once the Chosen few are gone, there will be nothing left to stop these jerks from settling the probabilities of the mortal realm and snipping off humanity once and for all from the great Pool of Time. After that, it's a simple matter to repurpose the energy of this universe, as if it never existed. No pressure kids!

Keep vigilant,

-Mr. Gray

A Little Stabbing

Channie stood with her hands on her hips as Steph stormed off in a huff. Channie knew she'd been sharp with her, but that was no excuse for Steph to call her names.

The nerve!

Channie was a straight shooter. There was no beating around the bush with her. It wasn't Channie's fault that Steph grew up privileged and didn't even recognize it! It was about time somebody told her that she'd been living a life on easy mode and most people didn't have it so lucky. Steph's whole personality seemed to be built around her self-entitled small town upbringing.

Admittedly, Channie didn't know Steph all that well, but the way she'd picked on Rebecca at camp was enough of a reason for Channie to dislike her. She was too worried about her mom to care about whether or not Steph's feelings were hurt. They weren't friends. Steph was just the mean girl at camp as far as

Channie was concerned. If anyone deserved to have a crap day like today, it was Steph, not Channie.

No one deserves this craziness....

Channie sighed. She knew she was just diffusing her worries through her bristly attitude. She could tell Steph was crying when she turned away. Channie didn't feel great about that. Steph's fragility surprised her, though perhaps it shouldn't have given the events of the day. She just didn't feel like Steph had been through it as hard as she, herself, had. The Dreadnaught didn't pry its way into Steph's mind like it did with Channie. She'd been convinced she was about to die. There was still a lot for her to unpack.

The elevator dinged down the hall. Steph was off to find food. Channie's stomach growled. She was too sick with worry to think about eating despite her stomach's protest. It had been a long night and day since leaving camp.

Channie returned to her seat and sat back down. It had been awhile since she'd seen any hospital staff. She hoped someone would give her an update on her mom soon.

On the other side of the waiting room, a white boy in an orange reflective work vest walked in from outside. His gaze fell across Channie and locked on to her in an instant.

Channie narrowed her eyes as the boy hurried towards her. He was slightly older than her, and the first thing she noticed about him was that he was very strong. She bit her lip subconsciously as she observed his large biceps through his dirt stained shirt. The boy's eyes held a strange intensity as he continued his hastened beeline in her direction.

The realization that the boy had a sword latched to his belt screamed cosplay nerd, but Channie wasn't entirely not into it. Her curiosity quickly turned into concern, though, when the boy, still halfway across the waiting room, pulled out what looked to be a steak knife from under his vest and ran at her like a psycho killer!

Channie screeched in surprise and held her hands up in front of her as the boy lunged on top of her. There was nothing she could do to deflect his attack. She was in such shock that she barely felt anything as the blade drove cleanly through her palm and out the back of her hand.

The boy jumped back immediately after stabbing her, leaving the knife imbedded in her palm. He looked almost as shocked as Channie. "I'm so sorry," the boy said, "I had to do that, you'll understand later."

Channie held her stabbed hand up to her eyes, dumbfounded as she stared at the protruding blade. The pain hit her a moment later, delayed along with her slow comprehension. "You stabbed me!" she cried out.

"Shhhh," the boy had the audacity to shush her. "I know I did. It had to be done. You'll be fine, I practiced for a long time so I could avoid all the tendons and arteries. You know, I didn't appreciate how complicated the human hand is until I found out I had to stab you through yours without leaving lasting damage. You are Channie, right? I probably should have confirmed that first…."

"YOU STABBED ME!" Channie screamed once more.

"Again, very sorry about that. I'm Landon, by the way. Lewis's friend…."

Channie could barely focus on the boy's words. Her hand felt white hot and freezing cold simultaneously as her nerve endings fired off in a panic. The first drops of blood only now began to seep from the wound.

The boy grinned sheepishly at her. The juxtaposition between his charming demeanor and the attack he had just committed against her was confusing for Channie, to say the least. With her fight or flight response triggered, Channie hadn't fully been able to absorb what was going on or figure out whether or not she was still in danger. There was excitement in Landon's eyes. His expression set off a chain of chemical events that lit an ember inside Channie. She tingled breathlessly under his gaze.

Landon reached out suddenly and gripped ahold of the knife's handle. He pulled it from her in a swift movement that immediately hurt ten times worse than it had on the way in. Channie's vision went white around the edges. The color changed to red as she squeezed her eyes shut.

When she opened them again, Landon was grimacing at her. "A time traveling journal told me I had to do that, and I always do what the journal says. It's like a blueprint to get to the correct future where we don't all die. So again, I'm very sorry about the stabbing."

Blood poured freely from both sides of the wound. Channie whimpered a pained cry. Landon shrugged a backpack off his shoulders and fished out a roll of gauze that he had preemptively opened and gotten ready for the occasion. He wrapped it expertly around Channie's hand and secured it with a metal clip.

"Why?" Channie asked between whimpers.

Landon swung his backpack back over his shoulder. "We need the bloody gauze to lure the zombie-vampire guys into following us back downtown to where time is frozen."

"What 'zombie-vampire guys'?" Channie scoffed.

"Several people already died from ghast bites. Once they die, they rise again and want to drink blood. You can ask your friend, Steph, all about them when she gets back up here." Landon extended his arm, offering to pull Channie up from her seat.

She wiped her eyes with the back of her sleeve before accepting his assistance. Somehow, no hospital staff had been alerted by any of her cries.

Landon continued once Channie was on her feet. "Now the trouble is, once they bite someone the disease spreads. The bit person soon dies and then they turn as well, unless they can be helped the way Mr. Gray saved Rebecca, which they can't because no more of that serum exists in our universe at the moment and the Agares have banned all travel to our universe from within the Beyond. We don't want to have a zombie-vampire den in Edmonds, so we have to take them back to ground zero with us so we can take care of everything all at once. All clear?"

"Hol' up, Norman Bates," said Channie, anger growing inside her to mask the pain. "Why the *hell* am I roped up in all this nonsense? Why not get someone else to deal with the Agares? Like an adult. Call the police, or the military, or Chuck Norris, just not me. What did I do to deserve all this?"

"'Why me?'" mocked Landon. "Are you really asking 'Why me?'—have Lewis and Mr. Gray explained nothing to you?"

Channie glowered darkly at the rude boy.

"It has to be us. We are Chosen. And I don't mean like Jewish 'Chosen People' chosen, I mean that cosmically we have been fortunate enough to be gifted with the power of choice. It's rare, but some people like us have destinies that are not set in stone the way it is for most of humanity. We are the uncertainty in the universe. The Agares wants to Erase all of the Chosen people throughout history so that they can settle our timeline and then cut the cord entirely. Erasing us is like turning off the power before cutting an electrical wire. Can you walk and talk?" Landon gestured for Channie to accompany him towards the elevators.

Channie followed behind him dubiously.

"We can't run from the Agares forever," said Landon. "Better to face them head on. I know you want to run away, drive off to Spokane, or Mexico, or somewhere farther, but after all of the trouble the Parcae took to bring our little group of Chosen ones together, we really do owe it to them to follow the journal through to the best of our abilities. And if that means stabbing someone sometimes when the moment calls for it, so be it. I know you're going to be mad at me for this for a while, but I stand by the decision."

"We're in a hospital," said Channie. "There has got to have been an easier way to get zombie-vampire bait than by maiming me."

"I'm not the QB of this game. I'm just following the plays as they're called."

They came to a stop in front of the elevator bank. A moment later, one of the elevators opened and Steph burst out winded and disheveled. "There are monsters in the basement," she said, shaking as she gasped for breath.

"We know all about that already. I'm Landon, Lewis's friend." He extended his hand for Steph to shake.

Steph blushed as she took Landon's hand in hers.

Channie felt herself quickly growing annoyed as she watched the exchange. Her throbbing hand didn't help her suppress her emotions either.

Landon took his bloody knife back out and wiped it on another piece of gauze before dropping it to the ground. "Breadcrumbs for the monsters to follow," he said. "Come on, let's go, I have my scooter parked in a loading zone."

No one tell Channie or Landon, but the real reason that stabbing needed to happen wasn't actually to obtain bloody gauze. Channie was right, finding a bag of blood in a hospital isn't that hard. In other timelines, that's exactly what they do—Landon just grabs a bag on the go. No, the true reason the journal told Landon to stab Channie was so that she would be left with a gnarly scar to remind her of just how bad Landon is capable of hurting her. The way Channie goes into all of her future interactions with Landon is forever colored by this first meeting. She doesn't really know what he is capable of, and that uncertainty makes Channie nervous. It's not a great place for any relationship to start, but it's all necessary for them to get to the end in one piece.

Keep vigilant,

-Mr. Gray

CHAPTER

26

Primal Hunger

As the shock of being stabbed through the hand wore off it was replaced by a searing ache. Channie's whole arm pulsed with her heartbeat as blood continuously spilled into the wrapping of gauze.

Landon was more convinced of the necessity of Channie's trauma than she was. The pain made it hard to even think. Silent tears formed in her eyes as she stumbled lightheaded behind Landon and Steph. Channie felt like chopped liver as Landon's attention zeroed in on Steph and never came back.

Admittedly, Steph did look more pale than usual, having experienced some sort of fright in her brief moment away from the hospital lobby, but Channie could hardly believe whatever had happened to Steph was worse than being stabbed by a stranger out of the blue. Landon seemed to just expect her to get over it.

Channie stopped walking momentarily as the wooziness turned her legs to jelly.

"Hurry up," said Landon, voice void of sympathy.

Channie leaned against the wall to steady herself. She shot Landon an unmissable glare.

Landon stopped when he realized Channie wasn't going to start walking again immediately. He frowned slightly as he observed the bright red spots forming in the gauze on both the front and back of Channie's hand.

The classically attractive boy unzipped his backpack and pulled out another strip of gauze. He lifted Channie's damaged hand gently in his own. Channie grimaced from the pain his touch caused, but allowed him to continue. Landon's expression softened as he unwrapped the gauze and took in his handiwork once again. He moved like a trained nurse, quickly wrapping the fresh gauze in its place.

Landon's gentleness surprised Channie after the aggressiveness of the stabbing.

"Here," he said, shoving the bloodied gauze into Channie's good hand. Next, he pulled a pair of surgical shears out of his pack and stuffed them into her hand as well. "I'm going to need you to cut off squares as we go, one every hundred yards or so. The vamps will follow, they're like sharks with blood."

Channie wasn't sure why Landon's lack of empathy for her pain bothered her so much. He was a stranger to her, but she just felt like he owed her better treatment after causing her such distress.

Down the hall, the elevator dinged again, stopping on the ground floor. Landon's expression became distant for a moment. "It's time to run…" he said, snapping back to his surroundings.

A terrified scream sounded from around the corner behind them. It ceased suddenly.

Steph bolted down the corridor without looking back, fear pushing her onward as fast as her feet would carry her. Landon grabbed Channie by the elbow and yanked her forward with him. The slap of footsteps against the linoleum sounded from the direction of the elevators. Channie didn't have to look back to know they were being chased.

The lights in the hallway began to flicker. Another scream started and quickly ended in a gurgling cry.

"Faster!" pleaded Landon.

Channie stumbled over her own feet, her body faltering in her weakened state.

She chanced a glance back as they reached the waiting room. The hallway had gone mostly dark behind her, but she could distinctly make out three dark shapes moving in pursuit. Only one of their pursuers was on the floor—the other two defied gravity, scampering along the walls and ceiling like berserk monkeys through a canopy.

Channie screamed as she nearly tumbled over a chair in the waiting room. Landon pulled her onward in his own panic.

Steph reached the door first, tripping the motion sensor.

"To the left!" Landon yelled up to Steph. He threw the key to his scooter at her.

Steph snatched the key out of the air and dipped left as she passed through the doorway.

The reanimated ghost victims moved with singular intention: To consume warm blood. Channie's pulse pounded in both her ears and her damaged palm as she stumbled forward. She was starting to feel faint. They were barely to the door when her vision began to slip. The corners of her sight darkened, closing in around the edges. Channie felt herself tumble over her feet in slow motion, almost as if she were dreaming. The all-too-real implications horrified her as her body failed.

She hardly even felt the ground as she bounced against the concrete of the walkway.

Her eyes were suddenly pointed back into the hospital. The 'Vamps' as Landon called them, had reached the waiting room. They crashed through the furniture, sending the flimsy chairs flying in every direction. Their faces remained dead focused on Channie—black eyes never blinking; expressions of primal hunger.

A puttering engine sparked to life nearby. The sound was muffled in Channie's ears. She felt dazed as a wobbling sensation rippled through her body.

Before she realized what was happening, Landon was pulling her back up to her feet. The engine sounds drew nearer. Steph, with a big white helmet that looked like a smooth bowling ball on her head, whipped into view driving a yellow Vespa scooter. The tires screeched as she made a sudden stop in front of Channie and Landon.

"I don't know how to drive this thing!" cried Steph.

"You're doing great!" said Landon as he climbed on behind her and practically dragged Channie up onto the tiny bumper of the scooter, facing backwards. "Just go!"

They lurched forward as Steph twisted the throttle. The cold expressions on the vamps' faces never changed as they continued moving towards the children at a full sprint.

"You dropped the gauze and scissors didn't you?" asked Landon, over his shoulder.

Channie had in fact dropped everything in her fall.

Landon didn't need her answer. He unzipped his backpack, which he already had held at his side and withdrew a second pair of shears. "I always take precautions."

Channie gasped as Landon placed the new pair into her injured hand—her other hand was too preoccupied with holding on to the Vespa for dear life. They turned out of the hospital parking lot, cutting through the thickening mist at dangerous speeds.

The sputtering moped was just barely able to outpace the frighteningly fast vamps. Channie hardly had time to breathe a short-lived sigh of relief before she noticed more creatures scampering across the rooftops of the buildings on either side of the street.

Landon awkwardly hooked one of his arms around Channie's anchored arm. "You can lean against me with your elbow," he said. "You'll need both hands to cut up your bandage."

Channie gulped down a thick glob of saliva. She tried in vain to steady her heart as she let go of the Vespa entirely, relying on Landon's support to remain balanced. She grabbed the scissors out of her other hand and began fumbling to remove her fresh bandage. Fortunately—or not, depending on how she looked at it—the bandage was already soaked through with more fresh blood.

This boy better not bleed me out.

A whole line of ungodly things followed in their wake, screeching and growling, barely visible in the mist.

Channie began dropping little bits of gauze like a toddler with a fistful of construction paper. It felt an awful lot like dumping chum on her own feet before swimming in shark infested waters. Passing the bloody morsels only seemed to invigorate the vamps amongst the gathering crowd of beasties.

Steph swerved around a parked car, continuing at a dangerous clip deeper into the fog. They had to slow down after Steph nearly ran into a mailbox. They had only barely established enough of a lead that Channie lost sight of the monsters in the mist.

"Keep dropping bits," ordered Landon. "Everything has to follow us." His voice was dead serious.

Channie complied, even as her vision began to slip again from the blood loss. She breathed deeply to steady herself.

The road shifted—they were suddenly going down a steep hill. Steph was driving completely blind now as the dense clouds enveloped them in a sea of white froth.

"Just let it roll," said Landon as he reached up and turned the key to stall out the engine. The Vespa went silent as they descended through the billowing clouds.

Channie ran out of gauze as the lengthy downgrade leveled out and the scooter coasted deeper into the strange hot plumes. To Channie, it felt like hell itself. The wet heat made her face sticky.

Channie's skin suddenly went clammy cold. She'd simply lost too much blood. As she lost consciousness, her slumping body threw off the weight distribution on the Vespa. Steph clipped the curb a moment later, and all three children were bucked off, tumbling through the air in despair.

The horde descends into the mist just as Landon intended, but nothing is easy when you're being hunted by beings with superior agility and singular intent. So many lives affected by the Agares' will....   Years later, Mrs. Davis refuses to acknowledge this day even happened. To her it was all a bad dream, with a lingering hospital bill. The funny thing about most adults is that even when something happens right in front of their faces, if what they experience doesn't fit into their world view, they will find all sorts of creative ways of explaining it away so that they can ignore it. People will often do this when confronted with terrifying possibilities, but the most terrifying possibilities are those that don't care whether you believe in them or not. That is to say, monsters exist, even if you close your eyes. Remember folks, existence doesn't rely on perception, only survival does!

Keep vigilant,

-Mr. Gray

CHAPTER

27

Dumpster Diving

Steph landed hard on her head against the curb. The helmet saved her life, she had no doubt! Her ears rang from the strike. She attempted to stand but a spell of dizziness pulled her back to the pavement.

Landon appeared by her side in the mist. "Are you okay?" he whispered.

Steph gazed up at Landon as her vision continued to spin. "I think so," she said, though her back ached from the fall.

Landon grinned nervously at her as he extended out a hand. Steph accepted, interlocking her fingers with his. His hands were rough but warm, and way bigger than her own. He pulled her up effortlessly.

Steph found herself an inch away from Landon's chest, staring up into his eyes. She felt her cheeks grow warm as she blushed. The thought of blushing made her blush even harder.

Landon's pupils widened as he observed Steph's emotion. His own cheeks became flush a moment later.

He's blushing too!

His reciprocation fueled Steph's confidence. She raised an eyebrow, reveling in their mutual attraction. An unexpected find amongst the insanity of the situation. The adrenaline coursing through Steph's veins made everything feel electric. She wasn't sure she'd ever felt as alive as she did right now.

A not-too-distant cry that sounded like a young child stole their attention in the next moment.

"That's a ghost," warned Landon. "Quick, help me move Channie."

Steph searched the dense fog for the girl. It took her a moment to spot her. Channie was unconscious on the ground, only about fifteen feet away, but already Steph could barely see her in the dense mist. She stumbled after Landon as he went to Channie's side, her equilibrium still a bit wobbly. Despite Steph's balance issues, she moved under Channie's left arm as Landon hefted her upright.

"This way," said Landon, dragging Channie off to the side of the road. The tips of Channie's sneakers dragged against the concrete between them as they moved.

A growl from down the street made Steph's stomach drop. Landon matched Steph's accelerated pace. She was struggling; she knew she wouldn't be able to keep carrying Channie for long.

"There, the dumpster," said Landon. "It'll mask our scent."

Steph frowned at the idea, but Landon didn't give her a chance to object. He threw open the plastic lid and then hefted Channie up into his arms with a grunt. He slid her over the lip of the dumpster, where she fell onto a pile of black trash bags.

He jumped in right behind her and then turned around to assist Steph in her climb.

The smell of garbage hit her in the face like a wet sock.

"Just get in!" pleaded Landon with an airy hiss.

A chuckle that sounded almost like a turkey gobble hastened Steph's resolve. She dove headfirst into the dumpster.

The stench enveloped her as her weight released the rotten air from the bags beneath. Landon didn't hesitate as he quietly dropped the lid in place over their heads. A tiny crack where the lid of the dumpster wasn't quite flush with the rim let in only the tiniest amount of light.

Something wet leaked onto Steph's ankle. The bags crinkled as she moved slightly. Landon's hand reached out and grabbed her sharply. Steph couldn't see him in the dark, but his message was clear: *Shut up.*

Steph held her breath as she heard a chittering from nearby— something was in the alleyway. She leaned slightly, trying to see out the crack, but her range of vision was only the space directly in front of the dumpster.

Channie moaned quietly beside her, still unconscious.

Steph could feel Landon's tension.

"Come here," called a voice that sounded eerily like her own. "Hey, come quick! Come here! Come help me!"

Landon's fingers dug into Steph's arm painfully.

After a hauntingly long moment of silence, something on all fours scampered past their hiding spot. Most notably, it was not a ghost. It was the size of a large wolf, but hairless with smooth eel-like skin, black as tar, which glistened slightly in the dewy condensation of the mist. The creature moved without making any sound. As it went by, Steph noticed that it had hands like a human, with long, black, slender fingers and sharp nails. Its feet looked the same as its hands—long toes that gripped at the pavement as it ran by.

It stopped suddenly, barely in Steph's range of vision.

A maw of spiny teeth appeared as its jaw unhinged.

"Help me!" it cried, mimicking Steph's voice.

It swiveled back and forth—ear holes on the sides of its head listening intently for any response.

Steph held her breath.

Channie began to moan again, her unconscious body becoming aware of her pain. Landon shifted beside the girl, stifling the sound with his arm.

Steph's eyes remained locked on the monster.

It turned its head, looking straight back at her. "Over here guys!" it yelled. "Come quick!"

Steph's pulse pounded in her ears as her blood pressure spiked. She had to force herself to take a breath, but she was too frightened to make any noise. Her inhale came as a series of small quick gasps—she was hyperventilating.

The garbage bags rustled slightly beneath Channie. She was starting to regain consciousness at the worst possible time.

The monster pranced silently over to the wall of the building across the alley. Its hands gripped like a monkey's against the brick as it climbed with ease straight up the wall and out of sight.

After a minute of silence, Channie groaned again and attempted to sit up.

Landon shushed her as he held her down with his arm. "Don't move and be quiet," he whispered. "That wasn't a ghast."

"It sounded like me," said Steph, eyes staying glued on the crack. All remained motionless outside of the dumpster.

"It sure did," said Landon. "I have no idea what that was."

"It went straight up the wall...." A shiver ran up Steph's spine. Her eyes were starting to adjust to the lack of light. She could see Channie glancing around with a confused expression on her face.

"What's that smell?" Channie asked.

"I think we should make a run for it," said Landon, ignoring the question.

"It might still be up there," said Steph. She didn't like the idea of leaving their hiding place.

"We're really close to where time is frozen," said Landon. "We just need to move quick and stay quiet. There are lots of things hunting for us, but the journal told me to follow my instincts, and they are telling me that we need to get out of here and push forward."

Channie remained silent, still gathering her bearings.

The garbage bags rustled some more beneath Landon as he opened his backpack and began digging through it. "Here, put these around your necks," he said as he handed each of the girls what appeared to be an acorn attached to a piece of twine. "This will stop you from freezing when we get near the basilisks."

Steph blinked twice, processing the strangeness presented to her. She barely had time to string the cord over her head before Landon lifted the lid. Steph looked up, straining her eyes to see through the fog. She scanned the roofline of the building across the way. There was no sign of the unknown monster.

Steph cringed at the clamor that arose as Landon climbed out of the dumpster. He hopped to the ground and unsheathed his samurai sword. It looked decorative, like a part of a Halloween costume. Steph wondered if it was even sharp. Landon held it up like a child posing while play-fighting as he searched his surroundings for threats.

Steph helped Channie climb out of the dumpster. Channie kept her maimed hand stiff at her side as she struggled to roll over the lip.

"Move out," said Landon in a hushed voice as soon as the girls were on their feet. His confidence did little to lower Steph's anxiety. She'd seen what was lurking. Landon stayed in the lead while Steph and Channie trailed behind. Channie was limping badly—her left leg had taken the brunt of her fall from the moped.

They continued on between the buildings and out into a small parking lot attached to the alleyway. Landon was moving a little too fast for Channie to keep up. Neither one of the girls were willing to call out to him as he rushed headlong into the dense clouds. They lost sight of Landon entirely as he entered a particularly dense plume.

Steph and Channie had to slow down even further as visibility dropped to nothing. Channie squeezed Steph's hand tight as they continued forward with careful steps. They could barely see the sidewalk beneath their own feet. Suddenly there was a change in the atmosphere. The gusting mist fell still.

Steph couldn't quite put her finger on what was different—the atmospheric shift was subtle. The stillness was obvious, though, and clearly unnatural. It felt repressive, requiring slightly more effort to breathe in the damp air.

As they walked deeper into the odd zone, the mist thinned slightly. They could see about fifteen yards ahead now. At first, there was no sign of Landon, but then a silhouette wandered across their path at the edge of obscurity. Relief turned to dread when Steph realized it wasn't Landon. The figure stopped mid-stride and turned towards the girls.

"Over here, help me!" the figure said. It sounded exactly like Steph.

Steph stopped, pulling back on Channie's arm as fear gripped her body.

The figure moved towards them quickly.

Steph fell backwards onto the ground helplessly. There would be no outrunning the creature.

Rather than the eel-skinned monster, Steph found herself face-to-face with her doppelgänger once again.

"It's okay," said Landon, appearing by their side. "It's just Clark."

Steph felt like she'd been kicked in the chest. Her heart hurt as she thought about her deceased father—also named Clark. The shapeshifter's fascination with her and her family was confusing and upsetting to Steph.

"Where are the others?" asked Landon.

"We must hurry," said Clark. The shapeshifter's skin rippled as it locked its eyes on Steph. The creature's body settled, slightly changed. It looked even more like her now, if that was even possible.

"Rebecca needs help," said Clark.

Landon held his sword behind him, to his side. "Lead the way," he said.

Clark nodded.

They all followed the shapeshifter deeper into the mist despite Steph's reservations. The day was feeling more and more like a bad dream as she watched her own ponytail bouncing along in front of her. A not-too-distant screech, possibly from a ghast, hardened the knot in her stomach. She wished she could be anywhere else in the world right about now.

There's nothing quite like the stench of garbage lingering in ones' hair at the end of a long day of trauma. Not a pleasant experience by any means, but certainly a badge of resilience. The stinky cherry on top. Steph took all of this very well, all things considered. She may feel unsettled by Clark's mimicry, but it really is quite the compliment. What's that human phrase? Imitation is the highest form of flattery. Clark has some telepathic abilities that help him in his shapeshifting craft. His mental receptors are tuned in on Steph. She'll learn to appreciate the sentiment of the gesture one day.

Keep vigilant,
-Mr. Gray

CHAPTER

28

Creepy Crawlers

The barrel of Josie's grandfather's rifle swung wildly into the air as Josie stumbled over a raised curb in the mist. She found herself in a parking lot. The visibility was so bad that she no longer had any sense of direction. The impenetrable haze was wholly disorienting.

She continued to breathe in the alien atmosphere tentatively as she recovered from her misstep. The air dampened her skin, leaving it dewy to the touch. The humidity was repressive to her lungs. If any biological contaminants lurked, she had no idea. That possibility was too frightening to even think about. She took shallower than normal breaths, as if that would keep contagions at bay, though she was not under any such illusion.

Lewis couldn't be far away, but everything beyond Josie's immediate vicinity was lost to the mist. The one consolation was that she very much doubted anything else could see through the fog any better than she could. She kept the rifle held up, ready to blast a ghost if one stumbled across her. She was confident she could kill a small one, but the thought of the giant ghast she'd seen earlier terrified her. She imagined it would be like fighting a bear.

She stepped lightly across the parking lot maintaining silent foot falls. All noise was already dampened, either by the mist or by the fact that time was frozen here at the city center. Josie didn't have all the answers. The blanketing hush softened sharp noises with an effect similar to snow cover.

A silent figure poised beside a vehicle to Josie's left caught her by surprise. She turned the rifle towards the figure, only moving in closer after she determined that it was another person and not a monster. A middle-aged woman in a pantsuit stood frozen in place like a mannequin. Josie lowered her weapon. As she reached the woman's side, she could already make out more individuals frozen in place across the parking lot.

It felt like walking through a photograph. Everyone was unnaturally still, standing eerily in the mist. Josie maneuvered between them. Their expressions were all mundane—frozen while unaware of any of the dangers that surrounded them presently.

Josie paused as she spotted motion at the edge of her vision. Something was moving amongst the crowd. A dense cloud of mist hung at knee level, hiding the ground. Josie strained her eyes. She still couldn't make out what was moving.

A flash of black popped up several times from out of the fog. In the limited visibility it looked like a man-sized centipede. It moved quickly between the frozen people, crawling up each of their bodies in turn. Josie couldn't tell what it was doing to them when it reached face level. She wasn't keen to find out.

Her heart pounded in her chest as the creature lowered itself back to the ground, disappearing from sight. She wanted to run, but it was already too close. She held the rifle at her side, but kept her finger gently over the trigger. The clicks of the creature's feet against the asphalt drew nearer. It took everything Josie had to hold steady.

She knew it was coming up to her, but there was nothing she could do. The clicking grew louder until it was right at her feet. Josie was shaking slightly—adrenaline in her veins. She held her breath as the creature rose up into the face of a man frozen directly beside her.

Stubby insect arms gripped onto the front of his blazer while more appendages prodded at his frozen face. The man's skin moved like clay, remaining depressed where the creature exuded force. It felt all over with a dozen tiny limbs, poking into the man's eyes and nose. It pried open his jaw as far as it would go before squishing its insect-like face completely into his mouth and regurgitating something down his throat.

That can't be good....

The creature withdrew, leaving the man's jaw gaped wide in a mask of horror as it dropped back to the ground.

Josie knew what was coming next. She silently adjusted the tip of the rifle to point directly in front of her own face. The centipede creature's pincer arms gripped onto her jeans as it slid up her body. She wobbled slightly under the monster's weight as it stood up tall against her. Only now did she realize that the creature was at least three times longer than what she could see sticking out of the mist.

It fixed its black, emotionless eyes on her face as it began to prod at her. A hiss escaped its maw as it realized that she was not frozen like the others.

Josie pulled the trigger.

Crack!

The blast made her ears ring horribly. The elongated body of the monster flopped lifelessly to the asphalt. The bang echoed back to her off unseen buildings. Nothing within a mile could have missed the sound of the shot.

Josie ran deeper into the mist. She wanted to put as much distance as possible between herself and the parking lot. All the faces of the frozen people she passed had their jaws wrenched open.

"Josie!" someone called from behind her. It *sounded* like Lewis. She didn't know if she could trust her ears. Something had called to her in Yost Park earlier as well. Whether a mimic or Lewis, the voice had come from where she'd just fired off her shot. She questioned if Lewis would have really risked calling out to her. He couldn't have possibly expected her to respond.

The rifle needed to be reloaded. She knew how, but she'd never actually done it by herself before. She felt at the spare rounds in her pocket. She only had a handful—five or six. She gripped one between her fingers and attempted to shove it into the chamber opening. Her hand fumbled with the round, shaking uncontrollably.

She needed to take a deep breath to steady herself. She tried again, relief spreading through her as the round finally clicked into place.

Without warning, Josie's mouth was suddenly covered from behind. She was spun around by a pair of hands to find Lewis standing wide-eyed at her side. "That wasn't me," he whispered.

Josie had to settle her heart again. She was surprised that Lewis had managed to sneak up on her. Lewis kept quiet as he guided her over to the side of a building.

"Help me!" the mimic cried in Lewis's voice. "Josie! Help!" A bloodcurdling cry pierced the stillness.

Had Josie not known it was the mimic, she would have had no doubt that Lewis was being hurt horribly. The cries ceased suddenly and did not pick back up.

Lewis kept a tight hold on Josie's hand as he led her down the street. Josie gripped back on to him just as tightly. After another block, Lewis paused at the intersection. A line of frozen festival-goers marked the entrance to the Taste of Edmonds.

Boy, oh boy! Us Parcae are not averse to eating grubs, but that grabbler laying eggs was enormous! The worst part, in my opinion, is not how much bigger those creepy crawlers get when fully grown, but rather, how violent their reproductive process proves to be on the incubator hosts. Time being frozen is their only consolation for a fate most gruesome.

Keep vigilant,

-Mr. Gray

CHAPTER

29

The Master of Nightmares

"We're here," whispered Lewis.

"Now what…?" Josie glanced around the festival entrance. The ticket seller's mouth was gaped wide open like the people in the parking lot—another centipede monster deposit site. Josie's skin crawled at the reminder of that terror. "We are right beneath the hole in the sky, aren't we?" she asked.

Lewis nodded. "Ground zero. The Dreadnaught is close, according to what Landon said."

"What could the Dreadnaught possibly show us that is more frightening than what's actually happening?"

Lewis shook his head. He didn't have an answer.

"I don't want to go in there…." said Josie. They both stood in stoic silence. Beyond the entrance gate, a sea of frozen festival-goers stretched into obscurity. Josie could just barely make out a funnel cake booth through the fog. "I don't even know what a Dreadnaught looks like," she said.

"I believe you'll know it when you see it," said Lewis.

208

"And what about everything else? I dcn't have enough bullets for everything hiding in here."

Lewis nodded somberly.

"Okay, then," said Josie. Her worries were not eased one bit.

"I just do what the journal tells me," said Lewis. "Trust the plan."

Josie supposed there was a lot of power in that. The recursively generated directions made a script to a successful path forward, she hoped. "Landon said all of us were supposed to be here. We shouldn't be alone," she said.

"That is true." Lewis searched the fog, as if expecting company. "I don't think we should linger here, though."

Josie eyed the ticket seller once more. His face was twisted and dimpled like the others, molded into a grotesque mask by the giant insect's stubby legs.

"In fact, we really should keep moving… like now…" said Lewis. "This is the main entrance for the whole fairground. Everything has to move through here to get in or out. Ground zero." Lewis pointed at the ticket seller's dimpled cheeks. "That's messed up! Let's go!"

Josie let him grab her hand and pull her forward. She hated being so passive, but Landon had said that Lewis needed to trust his instincts. So far Josie's intuition had been aligned with Lewis's.

So far.

Josie's whole world had deteriorated into a living hellscape flush with nightmarish creatures. She didn't fault Lewis for that, but her life was certainly more complicated since meeting the boy. Ever since the deaths of her parents, Josie knew 'ground zero' was always destined to crash down on her. It had always just been a matter of when, not if. When a person's whole world collapses, it isn't hard to imagine it happening again. She felt like she'd been waiting for the other shoe to drop ever since that fateful car crash when she was nine.

The darkened sky suddenly lit up in a brilliant flash, electric blue—a silent lightning bolt cutting through the mist. They worked their way slowly through the crowd, passing each booth with an abundance of caution. The mist began to thin out as they reached the end of the row of food stands. Swirling winds touched down forming a vortex from high above. The winds picked up strength as the pair approached the civic center's covered stadium bleachers. Visibility increased to about one-hundred yards as they entered the vortex. The bleachers' structure loomed above them.

With the air substantially more clear than it had been since entering the mist, Josie realized they were in the eye of the storm. She still couldn't see the hole in the sky far above, but the larger fairgrounds were revealed to her.

An inflatable slide and bouncy house marked a children's play area beside a row of carnival style games. A stage had been built within a playfield in front of the covered bleachers and several other structures had been erected for a tightrope and trapeze high-flying exhibition. The thin towers had rungs like utility poles for performers to climb, though no one was up there at the moment.

The rock band they had heard earlier in the day was up on stage, frozen mid set, with a small crowd gathered on the grass in front of them.

The hairs on the back of Josie's neck stood up as she noticed movement at a funhouse in the children's area. Another blue lightning bolt streaked horizontally across the sky in a blinding flash. Josie grabbed tighter onto Lewis as she rubbed her eyes with her other hand. Something had moved across an opening in the funhouse structure.

"I saw something move over there," said Josie, pointing towards the funhouse.

Lewis paused, straining his eye across the playfield.

Another lightning strike flashed, this time actually colliding with the funhouse instead of just rolling between the clouds. All the lights on the structure turned on in an instant, coming alive along with its sound system. Carnival music cut the silence of the otherwise frozen fairground.

They stood staring fixedly at the funhouse for a moment, searching for more motion amongst the now flashing lights. Josie felt that something was very wrong—a sense of being observed gripped her. Her skin felt like it was crawling as she spun around.

The changes to her surroundings were subtle at first. A dark lump on top of a porta-potty lowered itself as she turned quickly. A plastic tablecloth in a nearby booth rippled slightly. Things were hidden all around the children, watching and waiting as they passed. Lewis was looking around more closely now as well. His eyes grew wide as he took in all the small movements edging in to cut off their exit.

The monsters were lying in wait. They became more brazen as they realized they had already been spotted. More dark shapes slithered out from every hidden crease and blind spot.

Every structure had held at least one. They came out from behind every tent and garbage can. Across the fairground the trap was sprung. The myriad of creatures approached slowly as Josie swung the tip of her rifle back and forth in a lame threat. There were far too many targets to defend against.

Several Agares stood like poles; pale, tall and lanky. They glowered at her with seething intelligence behind their dark eyes. They held back behind the ghasts and other odd entities, slinking forward like wild animals. The horde remained eerily silent in their approach.

"This way!" cried Lewis, pulling Josie forward towards the bleachers.

There wasn't really anywhere to go by Josie's calculations, but she backed away with Lewis. Josie doubted she would be able to get more than one shot off from the rifle before being overwhelmed. The threat of that one shot was the only thing standing between them and being mobbed. The horrors matched their pace, corralling them towards the bleachers.

Josie realized they were going exactly where the monsters wanted them to go. From all over the fairground, they closed in on three sides, leaving a singular path open to the children. Carnival music filled the air as they stepped up onto the bleachers. The creatures did not follow them into the stands. Instead, they encircled the whole structure, preventing them from leaving.

"What are they waiting for?" asked Lewis.

To Josie it was obvious. They had been herded to the stands from the start. They were exactly where the Agares wanted them—delivered to the Dreadnaught.

The air rippled with visual distortions all across the playfield between the bleachers and the stage. Where there had appeared to be nothing, a gigantic mass of black fur two stories tall suddenly fazed into view. A head the size of a Buick contained a mouth big enough to swallow them whole. Jagged teeth opened into a wide grin as the enormous monster stared at the children. It looked somewhat like a simple house cat, but it was large enough to eat an elephant. It was truly an apex predator.

"Dreadnaught?" asked Josie, her voice sounding in a whimper.

"Dreadnaught," said Lewis, a sad, defeated look spreading across his face.

The monster made no vocalization, but it spoke to them, directly into their minds.

Hello, children. Come to die, I see. Did you think that tiny rifle could end me?

The deep voice boomed through their skulls in a rattling vibration that made their teeth buzz.

Lewis's jaw dropped open in shock and despair.

What do you fear? Would you like me to show you?

Josie screamed in defiance. She fired directly into the monster's face.

A chorus of snorting laughter erupted from the Agares amongst the crowd of mostly non-humanoid creatures.

The Dreadnaught didn't even blink. Its massive basketball-sized eyes focused in on Josie with elongated pupils. Her limbs suddenly felt like bricks at her sides. She dropped the rifle as she lost control of her body. She fell back into a seated position on the bleachers, where she remained despite her will to move. She felt like she was bound in place, no longer the steward of her own body. She'd lost all agency, left completely helpless as the monster turned its focus on Lewis.

Your fears are pathetically small, boy. Afraid to die alone? Afraid to be meaningless? Afraid to love a girl who barely knows your face? To lose her? What a laugh. You are afraid to live the life you were given. Your importance to this universe will be its downfall.

The Dreadnaught shifted closer to the bleachers. It opened its mouth and roared at them with a deep, soul rattling bellow. "I SHALL EAT YOU BOTH."

Lewis wasn't locked in place like Josie. He tugged at her sleeve, trying to coax her farther up the bleachers, but she wouldn't budge—couldn't.

The Dreadnaught put its front legs up over the railing, moving with slow, methodic steps.

Where would you like to die?

It was toying with them.

A haze fell over the children's vision. The bleachers disappeared, replaced by the cement walls of a basement.

Perhaps here?

Lewis fell to his knees. His skin shriveled up, dehydrating like a mummy until he looked like leather and collapsed on his side.

You might as well have died here, trapped and alone. The voice shook with glee. *And what about you?*

The walls melted away, shifting into the dark of night. Snowflakes blew past Josie's face as she flew backwards through the air. She glided with broken glass all around her, moving in slow motion. It was the car crash that killed her parents, playing back to her in reverse.

She sank back through the windshield. The glass flew against her, reforming painfully around her as she burst into the backseat. Time reversed directions again, flowing normally, the moment before they slid into the truck.

"Josie!" her mother cried out. "What are you doing? Sit down!"

Her dad turned his head. "That's dangerous!" he cried out as he lost control of the vehicle.

The blinding lights of the semi filled her vision.

Everyone you love dies because of you.

The collision launched her back into the air as her parents were crushed amongst the steel.

Josie cried out, overwhelmed with sorrow. She wished she could stay behind in the car and die with them.

The fairgrounds snapped back in place around her. Lewis was collapsed on his side at her feet. The Dreadnaught had turned away from them, something else having stolen its attention.

It took a moment for Josie to understand what was going on. Rebecca swung gracefully through the air above the goliath like a trained acrobat. She was holding onto the trapeze bar with one hand whilst gripping a glowing object in the other. Josie could barely see her, as she was almost lost in the bright white glow.

The Dreadnaught stood up on its hind legs, snapping its jaws at Rebecca wildly.

Josie's heart caught in her chest as Rebecca let go of the trapeze bar and flipped through the air. The light coming from the object in her hand grew with sudden intensity. Josie had to cover her eyes as the shine became unbearable. She felt like an explosion had gone off as the white light enveloped the entire fairground.

A cat should never be given so much power. Sadistic creatures, Dreadnaughts. These psychic psychopaths don't require much coaxing from the Agares to do their bidding. They enjoy making smaller creatures suffer. Once a beast like that witnesses the patterns of the multi-verse, there isn't much left to do but crush those that cross them into tiny balls of flesh and chew them up like bubblegum until they get bored and have to go find something else to torture. Real pieces of work. Dreadnaughts see other creatures the way small children see bugs—something to smash for no other reason than to listen to the sound they make when they pop. Meanwhile, I must say I feel somewhat responsible for Lewis's trauma with that basement. Back then, making him think I was going to leave him to die was simply the best way to push him forward on his journey. At some point he will have to stop obsessing over that. It's crazy how long claustrophobia can grip a kid, just from the threat of dying alone in an empty cement room. At least I still have Landon available to me for when I need someone to crawl into a tight or dark space for the good of the universe. Salvation comes from sacrifice.

Keep vigilant,
-Mr. Gray

CHAPTER

30

Time Eaters

Rebecca stepped confidently through the mist. She felt she could rely on her new sensory abilities to keep her safe. She knew the 'old her' would have been terrified to be in her current predicament, but the new Rebecca was unshakable. Such an odd experience to no longer fear anything at all. She didn't feel invincible, though she knew she was stronger and more agile than before—it was simply that the thought of death didn't worry her anymore. Death would come for everyone eventually; she no longer felt the need to fret over that fact. The new mindset was the biggest change she had undergone since contracting vampirism.

Josie and Lewis disappeared at her side as the mist thickened. She sensed no danger as she followed Clark into the dense cloud.

The next thing she knew, she was lying prone on the ground with a boy standing over her. The boy's hands were hovering around her neck.

Rebecca kicked up at him hard between his legs.

"Oooff," the boy grunted as he fell by her side.

Rebecca quickly took in her changed surroundings. Channie, Steph, and Clark—still disguised as a second Steph—were all standing off to her left. The differences between the two Steph's was obvious to Rebecca, though they certainly looked like twins to everyone else.

"Did I lose consciousness?" Rebecca asked. She stood down from her assault on the new boy. He continued to writhe around back and forth across the pavement beside her as she hopped quickly to her feet.

"Time is frozen here," said Channie. "That necklace Landon put on you unfroze you."

Rebecca's hand went immediately to a nut dangling from a string of twine around her neck. It was hardly the oddest thing that had happened today, but it was unusual. "And Josie and Lewis?" she asked Clark pointedly.

The shapeshifter bowed. "I protect you. They continue on."

Landon eyed Rebecca venomously as she extended a hand to help him to his feet. Rebecca matched his icy stare but kept her hand extended until Landon begrudgingly gripped onto her wrist.

Rebecca sniffed at the air as she pulled Landon up effortlessly. She could still faintly smell Josie and Lewis. Their trails were distinct, but partially dissipated. It was clear to her that it had been several minutes since they moved on from the area. There were other scents on the air as well—unfamiliar stinks that sent Rebecca's nostrils flaring with disgust.

"Things are near," she said. "We should move."

The other girls looked around wildly, eyes wide with terror. Rebecca smirked to herself. It was freeing to not hold any fear. Landon was staring at her. She sensed that he had been leading the group before.

Well, not anymore.

Everyone felt the shift of power—Landon submitted wordlessly, making things easier than she could have hoped. She could tell his feathers had been ruffled, but he knew what was good for him. Rebecca exuded alpha energy. She led the way forward without further discussion.

Rebecca couldn't explain exactly how she was choosing her path. It was like she was following a trail of energy. It drew her forward like the needle of a compass. The source of the energy was a mystery to her.

"You can sense them too," said Clark, sticking close to Rebecca's side. "The time eaters."

Landon frowned, peeking at her from behind Clark. "Are you talking about the basilisks? The giant lizards that are stopping the flow of time?"

Clark nodded. "They came to my world long ago. A moment turned into infinity. We all woke up slaves to the Agares."

Rebecca was surprised by how nonchalantly Clark spoke. *A whole world enslaved! How can we stand against an enemy that can stop time?* It was crazy to think that their little group was all that stood between the Agares and the end of the world. *No pressure....*

A distant tinkling of carnival music told Rebecca they were nearing the festival grounds. The music sounded even more twisted than usual as the pitch of the notes became warped by the strange swirling winds. Rebecca's heightened senses picked up another sound that nobody else seemed to have noticed yet: A clicking, chittering noise—dozens of tiny legs scampering across the pavement.

Rebecca proceeded cautiously.

Clark was the next to hear it. The shapeshifter's eyes bulged out farther than a human's naturally protrude. "A grabbler is near!" said Clark in a rushed whisper. "Stay still—it can sense movement and is mostly hairless."

Rebecca cocked an eyebrow at the odd description. Everyone stopped where they stood and remained in place as the chittering grew in volume to a level that was finally audible to the rest of the group. The mist was thick at their feet, hiding the *grabbler* as it approached.

Channie and Landon both had rightfully fearful expressions on their faces as they held in place. Steph, on the other hand, had a look of curiosity.

"What did you call it?" asked Steph, a little too loudly.

The chittering stopped momentarily, but then the silence was broken again by a hiss as the grabbler popped its head up out of the mist. Its gray, segmented insect body wormed into the air like a charmed snake, searching for the children with black, beady eyes.

"Ew," said Steph, a pinched expression on her face.

The grabbler dropped to the ground and scampered towards her with clicking legs and mandibles.

The look on Steph's face only turned to worry when the grabbler lived up to its name by grabbing onto her shirt and dragging her to the ground.

Clark sprang into action, human arms turning into tentacles as the shapeshifter lunged into the fray. Rebecca joined in as well, rushing to where Steph had just been standing. A muffled cry sounded from the mist at Rebecca's feet. She felt across the ground, searching for Steph in the dense layer of cloud. She latched onto what she hoped was Steph's leg and began pulling with all her might. Despite Rebecca's increased strength, Steph didn't budge under the weight of the grabbler and Clark combined.

She gave another useless tug before switching her approach. She wrapped her arms around the thick body of the grabbler itself. It was like grappling with an anaconda! Its body was hard to the touch, naturally armored, and made of almost pure muscle.

Steph lifted her head and cried out as they managed to pull the creature away from her face for a moment. "You said it was mostly harmless!" Her eyes were bulging out of her head.

"Mostly hairless," repeated Clark.

"Why would I care if it has hair or not?!" Steph gasped harshly.

Clark shrugged.

Landon pulled a taser out of his backpack. "Stand clear," he said as he jabbed at the massive insect. The click of the electric current buzzed loudly as a blue bolt arced between the device's electrodes. A second later, the grabbler received the zap. The monster immediately released Steph and slithered away even faster than it had approached.

Steph had definitely received at least part of the shock. She climbed back to her feet, rubbing her wrenched jaw with her fingertips. "It tried to put something in my mouth…."

"It wanted to turn you into a mommy!" said Landon.

"Incubator host," corrected Clark.

"Great," said Channie, "so the only creature here that doesn't want to kill us directly wants its babies to burst out of our chests instead."

"No," said Clark, "the babies eat you before coming out."

Steph gagged.

"You didn't swallow any eggs, did you?" asked Landon.

Steph eyes teared up. "I don't think so," she said.

"You would know," said Clark. His tentacles morphed back into human arms. "Big eggs."

"We should go before it comes back…" said Landon.

Rebecca helped Steph back to her feet. "Let's assume everything wants us dead from here on out," she said.

Steph grimaced, embarrassment finally settling in.

"What else do you have in that backpack?" Rebecca asked Landon.

Landon smiled without his eyes. "A sandwich bag full of Carolina Reaper peppers." He pulled out the baggie as he put away the taser. He began to hand out the ridiculously spicy peppers as if they were a snack.

Clark held one up to his mouth, but Channie smacked it away from him before he could eat it. "Are you crazy? That would burn so bad!"

Rebecca was fairly certain Channie was mistaking Clark for Steph.

"Just feed those to the basilisks if you get a chance," said Landon.

"Really?" asked Channie. "That's the best you have in there?"

"I also have wristbands for the festival, but I don't think the ticket taker is checking very hard with time being frozen and all." Landon gestured for everyone to follow him. "We won't be taking the main entrance in, regardless."

They continued on until they reached a strip of chainlink fencing that blocked their path forward.

"I can't climb that," said Channie, rubbing her leg.

"You don't have to," said Landon. He pulled a wire snipping tool out of his backpack and got to work on the fence.

Rebecca could feel the presence of the basilisks ahead. She didn't like the idea of being armed with only a pepper. As soon as Landon had snipped enough links he pried back the cut section and everyone filed through one at a time. When Rebecca leaned over to slide through the gap, Landon whispered in her ear: "It's fine if you want to keep leading the group—the basilisks are over by the cornhole competition area."

"Is that what your journal tells you?" Rebecca asked. "Lewis told me about your instructions."

"Yeah," said Landon, "it's yet to steer me wrong."

"I suppose that would be what would happen," said Rebecca. "I mean, the journal was created by countless versions of you boys trying every possible combination of events until something worked, right?"

"I mean—" started Landon.

"—So each previous version probably had everything work out just fine, that is, until something didn't, and somebody ended up dead or something, and then they would go back and change the journal to work around the problem. What if the problem that kills us hasn't been solved yet?" Rebecca stared Landon down.

"I mean, yeah, that's how it works I guess, but we have a system. If I was to edit something in, I would mark the instructions as having never been attempted before, that way a future me would know when to improvise if necessary." Landon wrung his hands together. "I've never had to add anything before, personally, but that's what I told myself I would do, anyway."

Landon tried to follow Rebecca through the gap, but she shifted her weight and blocked the opening once more. "What else did your instructions say about today?" she demanded.

Landon matched her dead-eyed stare with a frown of his own. "After warning of basilisks at the cornhole area, it just says one thing: 'Let Rebecca do what she does.'"

Rebecca grabbed Landon by the front of his shirt and pulled him through the fence to her side. By the scent of fear seeping from his pores, Rebecca could tell Landon was feeling more than a little uneasy. "Sounds like past-you knew what was good for him," she said. "Stay out of my way." The vampirism was definitely affecting her demeanor. She knew there was no reason to be mean, but she was also glad to put

Landon in his place. He was just another boy with a savior complex as far as she was concerned. She knew she was being harsh, but she didn't really care.

"Come on!" said Channie. "What's taking you guys?"

Rebecca pushed past everyone, following the tingling feeling in her mind that Clark said was her sensing the basilisks. The mist thinned as they crept deeper into the fairgrounds. She could smell other things on the air long before visibility cleared up enough for her to see them.

A large stadium bleacher structure was surrounded by all sorts of nasty monsters. Clark stepped up to her side and pointed at the towering shape in front of the bleachers. "Dreadnaught."

Rebecca was taken aback by how large the creature was, easily standing two-and-a-half stories tall—her eyes didn't want to believe it at first.

"It's a friggin' space cat!" exclaimed Landon.

Rebecca glared at him. "And you're telling me everything is up to me? I have to figure out how to take that thing down?"

Landon was as pale as a ghost. "I didn't know it was so big…."

"Umm… guys?" said Steph. "My necklace is glowing."

Landon's head turned back around towards Steph so fast that Rebecca wondered if he might have given himself whiplash. "You gotta get rid of it!" he cried. "It's gunna blow!"

Rebecca felt the tug of fate drawing her forward like a hook behind her navel.

"When that thing goes off, we aren't going to need the Carolina Reapers!" exclaimed Landon. "If basilisks 'eat time,' then this thing DEVOURS it!"

The sickly sweet stink of fear became overwhelming in the air around Rebecca as everyone else sweated out their emotions. They all turned, staring fixedly at Steph as the nut on her necklace began to glow brighter.

"How am I supposed to get rid of it?" asked Steph. "Won't I freeze if I take it off?"

Rebecca followed the tug of fate as she ran up to Steph and ripped the necklace from her. She could feel heat radiating from the glow. The moment the necklace pulled free, Steph froze in place, just as she had anticipated.

Rebecca turned around, immediately eying a pole with a trapeze bar hooked at its top. Its placement was conveniently above the towering Dreadnaught. She made a beeline for the structure, running as fast as her agile feet would carry her.

None of the amassed monsters around the bleachers noticed her approach—at least none turned her way. The glow from the necklace intensified. Time was running short. When she reached the pole, the nut was already starting to blind her with its shine. She placed the cord of the necklace into her mouth and bit down hard to hold it from falling as she climbed.

With eyes closed to save her vision from the glow, Rebecca gripped onto the hooked rungs of the pole's ladder with both hands and climbed like the universe was depending on her. It wasn't until she reached the top that she snatched the necklace out of her mouth with her right hand, while simultaneously grabbing the trapeze bar with her left. She yanked it loose, and without a moment of hesitation jumped from the perch.

Rebecca flew through the air above the hulking beast with the greatest of ease. The nut was glowing so brightly that she had to squint to make out the snapping jaws at her feet. She followed her instincts, releasing from the bar and tumbling haphazardly through the air as she took aim at the Dreadnaught's gnashing teeth.

"Take that, Space Cat!" Rebecca screamed as she chucked the glowing nut straight into its gaping maw.

The Dreadnaught exploded into white light.

I warned you about the Gobu nut.... What a brilliant display of energy! The Dreadnaught didn't see it coming, not at all! That was about a thousand years of built up energy collected into a single point—a mini singularity—blasting off all at once. A holy hand-grenade! Just wait until you see what grew out of the stump of the Dreadnaught's body! The funny thing about the Gobu tree is that it doesn't grow in just one direction in time. Everyone who was frozen while it sprouted will suddenly see it appear, but instead of being confused by its presence, they will all remember the tree as having always existed in that spot. Its roots drink time, not water, and they establish themselves in the past and future simultaneously. It even twists up my mind to think about it. Sometimes you just have to accept that something exists and move on. Just don't drink the sap. That stuff will give you diarrhea so bad you'll feel it yesterday.

Keep vigilant,

-Mr. Gray

CHAPTER

31

Loose Ends

Landon shielded his eyes with his arm as white light exploded from the Dreadnaught's mouth. When the blinding brightness finally faded, Rebecca and all of the monsters were gone. An old tree with gnarled roots and knotted branches stood where the Dreadnaught once towered.

Time was flowing normally again. Children laughed at a nearby bouncy house. The band on stage jammed on. No one batted an eye at the ancient-looking tree, growing up in such an odd position between the bleachers and playfield.

Steph had a confused look on her face. "I can't remember why we're here," she said.

Clark was standing by her side, disguised as an older white man now.

Channie looked at Steph and then back at the massive tree. "Your nut sprouted," she said, pointing up in dismay.

Steph squinted questioningly.

A tug at the back of Landon's knee brought his attention to Mr. Gray, suddenly by his side. "Everyone who was frozen when the Gobu nut sprouted has memories of it always being there," he explained with a twinkle in his eye.

"Where's Rebecca?" asked Channie.

Mr. Gray's face became more stoic. "She was too close," he said. "Josie and Lewis were too near as well. Every entity that wasn't frozen in time has been spirited away, whisked across space and time. They have their own journeys to attend to—as do we!" Mr. Gray rummaged through Landon's backpack and retrieved the entrance bracelets for the festival. He passed them out to Clark and the girls. "You'll be safe here, today. All the baddies are scattered."

"So we won?" asked Channie. "The Dreadnaught is gone?"

"Yes, yes," said Mr. Gray. "I've just said that, haven't I? Now won't you three go enjoy the festivities, monster-free, while I take Landon to go tie up some loose ends?"

Steph still looked confused, but Channie took the dismissal in stride. They stuck with Clark as he wandered off towards the cornhole toss area.

Mr. Gray led Landon off behind a row of booths. The Parca gestured broadly towards the festival-goers. "They'll never know all you've done for them," he said. "So much goes unseen. It feels bad at times, being unnoticed, but it's also the best-est of defenses!"

Landon knew that the Parcae as a species were invisible to humans unless they chose to reveal themselves. The festival-goers walked right past Mr. Gray without seeing or hearing a thing. "So, what are we doing?" Landon asked the little imp.

"Loose ends—I already said that as well," said Mr. Gray as he felt at the breeze with his fingertips. He could see things that Landon could not; swirling energies stretching between worlds like strands of gooey cheese.

Mr. Gray tugged at one of the invisible strands and the light deadened across a plane, forming the square outline of a portal to the Beyond. "Don't worry, I'll bring you back here when we are done, and you can spend the rest of the summer getting to know your new friends."

Landon smiled to himself. Steph and Channie certainly weren't hard to look at by any means. He reveled at the chance to get to know them better under less stressful circumstances.

Mr. Gray disappeared into the portal. Landon breathed out as he stepped through the threshold and felt the world slip away. The conduit was like a tunnel. Energy swirled around him, disorienting his senses as he forged forward. It wasn't until he emerged on the other side that he allowed himself to breathe in again. The air was hot here. He was in the space between places. The Beyond was a dark realm, at least to his human eyes. To the Parcae, with their superior bandwidth, the air was aglow with a torrent of fire—all the twisting energies of the multi-verse.

Mr. Gray hopped along in front of Landon at the base of a hillside. The ground was covered in loose, flat stones, chipped away like plates from a larger geological source. There was no plant-life to be found by the limited glow of the swirling energies high above. Countless colors twisted together in the sky, forming a shimmering aura.

Mr. Gray read the air once more with his fingertips, feeling for their re-entry point. He grumbled to himself as he looked up the hillside. "Be quick," he said, "the Agares were forced from Earth, but they still linger here."

Landon followed Mr. Gray as best as he could as the tiny Parca scampered up the loose stones. Several times Mr. Gray had to stop and wait as Landon slipped on the shards. Every little stumble sent expanding landslides tumbling downhill beneath him.

Mr. Gray's eyes flashed his way. It was clear what he thought of Landon's lack of dexterity. As they climbed higher, Landon noticed a red haze building along the horizon above them. The hot air shifted direction, and with it, smoke began to pour down the hillside. Nothing could have prepared Landon for what he saw when he reached the crest of the ridge.

They stood upon the edge of a smoldering crater at least a mile wide, and half a mile deep. Landon could only guess at its scale, as the fumes rising up from the hole distorted the atmosphere and blocked out his view of the other side. "What happened here…?" he asked, in awe of the view.

Mr. Gray stared into the noxious abyss silently for a moment before responding. "The Agares have powerful weapons. This was once a Parcae city. Perhaps some survived. Our tunnels run deep."

Landon paused with Mr. Gray for a moment to pay their respects above the flames. It was Mr. Gray who broke the silence.

"I can almost reach it from here," he said, eying something in the sky that Landon could not see. "Could you give me a lift?"

Landon grabbed ahold of the Parca by the waist of his patchwork jacket and lifted him into the air. He looked like a dapper toddler in his arms. Mr. Gray reached out and grabbed at the air. A portal materialized at his fingertips. The opening stretched into a tall rectangle as Landon placed the little imp back on the ground.

"Hold your breath or breathe out as you go through," said Mr. Gray. "I forgot to say that last time, so it's a good thing you happened to do so naturally—otherwise you would have been sick."

"The journal warned me," said Landon.

"That's good," said Mr. Gray without any inflection in his voice. He looked tired. His eyes were distant.

Landon couldn't fault him. He couldn't imagine how many Parcae had died in the Agares attack. "I have a maple bar in my backpack," he said. The journal had also suggested he pack the doughnut.

Mr. Gray extended his hands out as Landon dangled the grocery store pastry in front of him. He snatched it out of the air and consumed it quickly. When he was finished, he went on to lick the maple frosting off his fingertips, so as not to miss out on a single calorie. He gave Landon a nod before stepping into the Portal.

Landon took one last look at the crater before following him in.

The Agares are truly terrible….

He breathed out as he crossed the threshold. The tunnel of energy whipped around him as he forged forward. He knew they would emerge at a different time and place than where they'd left, but it was still jarring to see the night sky when it had just been mid-afternoon before. The edges of their exit portal exploded outwards, sounding in a loud pop like a car backfiring. Landon glanced around. They were in a suburban cul-de-sac. The street was dark and empty.

"You gunna tell me why we're here?" Landon asked.

Mr. Gray raised his thin arm and pointed across the street towards a dark house. "The man who sleeps there is known as The Magnificent Harold. He has been selected as the spectacle for the Taste of Edmonds. If he lives, there will be no trapeze bar for Rebecca to use to defeat the Dreadnaught. He is the worst man in your universe right now, because his thread stands in the way of success."

"What are you saying?" asked Landon, worry settling in like a punch in the stomach.

"Harold must die. And you're going to kill him!"

Landon sure wasn't expecting to need to become a murderer today! I don't mean to sound glib. I'm only excited because of how necessary this experience will be for his psyche. Landon needs to be merciless in saving the whole of humanity. He can't be letting one little magic-shop magician stand in his way if he is going to succeed—not when it comes to the fate of the universe. I feel empathy, but I can't help this. Sometimes sacrifices are required for the good of the whole. I'm sure Harold wouldn't agree, but such is life.

Getting in the grit for the sake of humanity,
-Mr. Gray

Continue reading for a special preview of:

Into the Beyond

Part IV : Fables & Terrors

Paul James Keyes

CHAPTER

1

Lost

An explosion of light erupted from out of the Dreadnaught's throat. Everything was lost to the light. Lewis's senses were overwhelmed. His stomach cramped painfully as if he'd received a knee to the chest. He felt like he was being twisted into a knot. Gravity shifted, tossing him skyward. He clung onto Josie's hands as they flew haplessly through the air, clueless as moths caught in the vortex of a bonfire. His muscles strained to hold on, but soon the forces became too intense. Josie was ripped from his arms. They fluttered like leaves on the wind, falling sideways, destination unknown.

The air became hot for a moment, but then a chilly blast struck Lewis's face. He twisted head over heels in a disorienting spin. His tumble ended abruptly as he landed hard on his back. The wind was knocked from his chest. He gasped for air as snow blasted up the back of his hoodie. It took a moment before he was able to catch his breath and then another before he could do more than moan out in pain.

The sky was bright, but the temperature was frigid. Lewis began to shiver immediately. He knew he was in grave danger, as improperly dressed as he was. When he was finally able to sit up, he found himself alone in a snow frosted valley. A dense forest stretched up embankments on either side of him. Unfamiliar mountains pierced the sky in the distance, snowcapped and jagged. The Agares horde, including the Dreadnaught, were thankfully nowhere to be seen, but Josie and Rebecca were absent as well.

A boom like a distant drum rang in a low rumbling tone. The ground shook. More booms followed shortly, reverberating across the valley. The sound was coming from the direction of the mountains and it was getting closer.

It wasn't until Lewis saw the distant canopies of the trees bending away from a central force that he realized the booms were the slow trod of a giant creature cresting the valley's wall.

Lewis felt his heart begin to race as the tips of the trees wrenched sideways. Whatever was bending them out of the way must have been even larger than the Dreadnaught.

Ahead of Lewis, at the treeline, a teenage boy wearing a muted green cloak burst from the foliage ahead of the approaching giant. He spotted Lewis and made a beeline for him. The boy shouted something at him, but he couldn't understand his language. It sounded Nordic to Lewis, but all he really knew was it wasn't English.

The boy gestured violently behind him at the ruckus and then ahead in a desperate motion. His meaning was clear:

Run.

Broken trees and rocks tumbled down the side of the valley.

Lewis turned and ran in the same direction as the boy, still ahead by a few dozen paces. As he entered the trees, his hips and legs were already aching, but the pain was dwarfed by his fear. Despite his resolve to flee, the boy quickly caught up with him. He grabbed Lewis under the arm and pulled him along even faster. He stayed at his side even as Lewis stumbled over the shaking ground. They continued on up the hillside, quickly losing their lead as the booms gained on them. The monstrous footfalls maintained their steady pace, but the sound grew steadily louder with every step.

At the crest of the hill, the trees suddenly opened up, revealing a sheer cliffside before them. An ocean stretched the horizon, choppy with winter swells that lapped against the rocky shore one-hundred yards below.

The cloak-wearing boy stopped on his heels. He put his arm out, holding Lewis back from tumbling over the drop-off. They turned to look at each other, breathing hard, hearts racing. The boy was dressed all in furs and leather. His beige tunic had a satchel hooked to its side. His eyes shone sapphire blue, wide with exhilaration.

He smiled at Lewis, despite Lewis's own face being twisted in terror. The boy reached his fingers into his pouch and pulled out a spherical stone, caved perfectly round like a marble. He said something Lewis couldn't understand, then turned slowly to face the rumbling monstrosity that was quickly approaching from behind.

Trees splintered in its wake, cracking like toothpicks under its massive weight. The boy tossed the stone at their feet. It immediately began to glow as it settled in the dirt. The trees exploded towards them as the massive monster broke through. The debris bounced away from them harmlessly—an unseen cushion of air protecting their bodies.

The boy turned to Lewis and grabbed him by the front of his hoodie. There was nothing Lewis could do as the boy tossed him like a sack of potatoes off the cliffside. He screamed as he fell to the mercy of the churning waters far below.

A Note from the Author:

If you enjoyed the novel, I also have another series I'm writing—The Arcadian Complex, featuring my debut novel, Wrought by Fire. The books are a lot longer in that series, as they are aimed at an older audience—a series where I don't hold back on the content. It was and still is a labor of love, and I consider it to be my masterpiece. The first two books are already complete as of this writing, with more to come between Into the Beyond releases. You can read the synopsis of Book 1 on the next page.

Also, please don't forget to leave a **review** online! That, along with telling your friends and family about my books, is the best thing a fan can do to give back. The more attention my novels get, the lower the financial burden of writing them will become (it takes years). I will continue to share my stories, one way or another, because that is what I love to do!

About the Author:

Paul Keyes was born and raised in Washington State between the beautiful waterways of the Puget Sound and the always majestic Cascade Mountains. Fascinated by the political and social workings of the world, he obtained degrees in both creative writing and economics from the University of Washington. In his spare time, he is an experienced pianist and composer, which has helped him bring a heightened sense of rhythm and emotional resonance to his written passages. Over the years, he has traveled everywhere from China to the Mediterranean, soaking in the many diverse cultures and histories. Throughout it all, there is no place he would rather be than back home, drifting on a boat somewhere between the San Juan Islands and his home port of Edmonds.

You can follow Paul on Twitter **@PaulJKeyes**,
TikTok **@PaulJamesKeyes**,
or visit **VergePublishing.org** to become an honorary Chosen!

Also By Paul Keyes:

The Arcadian Complex Series

*An Ancient Magic lingers from a Forgotten Era.
Wizards Reign & Terrorize with Godly Powers.*

Salvine is sold to a madman who uses her flesh to form a beast with an unquenchable **thirst for blood**. She must do as her master commands—fetch the head of the bearer of the *Mark of Kings*.

Her target, a man plagued with *haunting visions of a destroyed world*, discovers he can bend both man and nature to his will as long as the moon hangs in the sky. The symbol etched into his bicep is more important than he realizes. He is fated to be king, but only if he can survive a perilous journey across lands ruled by powerful tyrants.

When a local boy named Javic discovers the future king on his farm, he doesn't think his luck can possibly get any worse. If only he knew Salvine—the girl he **secretly loves**—is trapped in the mind of one of their hulking stalkers.

An epic tale of magic and mayhem spans a rich world brimming with danger.

You can find the series on Amazon, or visit the website, **ArcadianComplex.com**